THEIR VICIOUS DARLING

VICIOUS LOST BOYS BOOK THREE

NIKKI ST. CROWE

BLACKWELL HOUSE

ISBN 13: 979-8-9854212-9-3

Published by Blackwell House LLC

ACKNOWLEDGMENTS

This book would not be possible without the help of several readers.

We can all agree that in the original *Peter and Wendy*, the depiction of Native characters was extremely problematic. When I set out to do a Peter Pan retelling, it was important to me to keep the Native presence on the island, but it was of the utmost importance that it be done in the right way.

I have to thank several sensitivity readers for helping me portray the twins and their family stories in the *Vicious Lost Boys* series in a way that was accurate and respectful to the Native culture, even if the twins reside in a fantasy world.

So a huge thank you to Cassandra Hinojosa, DeLane Chapman, Kylee Hoffman, and Holly Senn. You were and continue to be extremely helpful and I appreciate you so much!

I would also like to thank Brianna for her invaluable feedback and guidance on the portrayal of the character of Samira "Smee" in *Their Vicious Darling*. Thank you, Bri, for your time, energy, and feedback!

Any mistakes or inaccuracies that remain in this book are entirely my own.

BEFORE YOU READ

The Vicious Lost Boys Series is a dark romantic reimagining of *Peter and Wendy*. All characters have been aged up and are 18 and over. This is not a children's book and the characters are not children.

Some of the content in this book may be triggering for some readers. If you'd like to learn more about CWs in Nikki's work, please visit her website:

https://www.nikkistcrowe.com/content-warnings

To all the girls who were ever afraid to embrace their dark side.

“Wendy, one girl is more use than twenty boys.”

— J. M. BARRIE

PROLOGUE

THE CROCODILE "ROC"

My preferred way to travel is with a royal family. Any will do.

Because royal families always travel in luxury.

The Darkland royals are no different—they're one of the richest in the Seven Isles and they spare no expense. But they're shit for travel companions. Unless I'm fucking them. Then they're all right.

Amara Remaldi, Her Royal Highness The Duchess of Gordall, youngest princess of the Remaldi family, finds me in the portside dining room.

"There you are," she says as she comes over.

I crack open a peanut shell, empty the contents into my mouth then toss the shell into a nearby ashtray.

She is excited to have found me, apparently. I can hear it in the upward lilt of her voice.

I suppose being buried nearly balls deep in her last night might have something to do with it. When she came for me, she quivered like a leaf.

Amara may be a princess but she likes being dominated and I like to make royals beg.

Keeps me looking young.

I crack another shell, then break the peanut between my sharp incisors. Amara winces.

"What is it?" I ask.

"Giselle and Holt wonder if you'll join us for dinner." She stops a few feet from me and clasps her hands behind her back. She's wearing the Remaldi black velvet with the rearing lion embroidered in gold on the breast of her tunic. She's more soldier than princess preferring violence over politics, but she's never seen a battlefield in her life.

There is a long sword at her waist. The hilt is encrusted in cabochon rubies, making it nearly impossible to wield on a good day.

The weapon is for show, a blatant display of wealth.

It says, *I'm so rich, I can make swords I don't use glitter and gleam.*

"Your sister just wants me to bend her over and pull her hair and make her feel like a dirty little whore." I abandon the peanuts and light a cigarette, then spread my arms out over the back of the ornate settee that is bolted to the ship's floor. The portside dining hall is only used on special occasions, but I'm special every day.

"Will you?" Amara asks me.

"Pull your sister's hair?"

She clucks her tongue. She's jealous of me fucking others at court. "*No*. Come to dinner."

I sigh and lean my head against the back of the settee. "I would prefer not to."

"Roc." Her voice purrs on the R.

"Yes?"

She comes over to me and climbs on my lap, straddling

me. I can feel the heat between her legs. The leather of her brand new boots groans as she settles in around my thighs. "Come to dinner, please."

Pretty princesses asking please.

There is nothing quite so *pleasing*.

Amara has the family's blond hair, but hers is curly. She keeps it straightened though, and pinned back most of the time to keep the rumors of her parentage at bay.

No one in the Remaldi family has curly hair.

But her father's Captain of the Guard did.

And there were definitely rumors of the captain having an affair with the Crowned Queen.

I take another hit from the cigarette. Amara's eyes sink to my mouth, to the way my lips pull on the paper. I let the smoke cloud out a second later, before I quickly suck it back in.

A little breath escapes her and she rocks against me, grinding her clit against my crotch.

But I'm in no mood.

Not when Neverland is drawing closer and my hour of need closer still.

"Come to dinner and I'll make it worth your while." She reaches between us to grope me.

Amara is arguably the least likely to rule, though I've been surprised before. After all, I thought a Lorne prince would currently be ruling over my homeland, and then my dear baby brother gutted the entire family with his bare hands. So...*surprise*.

But what Amara lacks in royal power, she more than makes up for in debauchery.

Before this nonsense, we were spending most nights in the Darkland Red Light District fucking and getting high until we couldn't see straight.

"I suspect you will be making things worth my while with or without dinner," I tell her and take another long pull on the cigarette. Her pale cheeks pink. I am far too old for her, even though we look the same age, which is twenty and six, give or take.

Probably I am far too old for half the people I fuck. Being immortal will have that effect.

"Sister wants to be sure your allegiance to us remains intact," Amara goes on, "and that you won't grow soft when it comes to your brother."

I sigh. "I have not spoken to, nor laid eyes on Vane in years. There is no ground between us to grow soft."

If Amara were adept at reading through her lust, she would know I was lying. I am pissed at my brother, *yes*. He chose Peter Pan over me. But would I betray him to the royal family? Never. Never in a hundred years.

So I have to tread lightly and I blame the fae queen for that.

After all, when she hailed for me, promising to reveal Peter Pan's secrets, she sent the letter to the palace knowing full well the royal family would intercept it and insert themselves into the cause. They've been looking for any excuse to get the Darkland Death Shadow back from my brother. They've just been too terrified to confront him.

No, they're hoping his terrifying older brother will do their dirty work for them.

But I suppose all of that will depend on what these secrets are that the fae queen is holding over my head.

If they are worthless, I will find something else to occupy my time.

If these secrets hold value...

I think Vane might have a hard time deciding which

side he lands on—mine or Peter Pan's and I think if he has a hard time deciding, I will decide for him.

I don't hate Pan. I don't like him either.

We had a good time, cutting off Hook's hand as punishment for what he did.

But good times are not the same as obedience and loyalty.

And I could never control Peter Pan, either blatantly, or surreptitiously. And he sure as hell would never be loyal to me.

Which means I automatically like him less.

"Come to dinner," Amara says again, edging on a beg this time.

I'm not getting out of this one, not when I'm stuck on a fucking ship.

"Fine."

Her teeth gleam beneath her satisfied smile.

I groan and pull out my pocket watch, checking the time.

"I'll have to leave early," I tell her. "No exceptions."

"You and your watch." She leans forward, drives against me again, and brings the wet swell of her lips to mine.

All right, maybe I am in the mood.

I grab her ass with my free hand. Her tongue flicks forward, chasing mine and the kiss deepens.

My cock hardens. Amara wiggles her hips, bringing the heat of her core closer to me.

Fuck.

And then she's gone.

My heavy eyes snap open to find her looking amused several steps back. "That's all you get for now." She drags the backside of her hand across her mouth. "Come to dinner. Then you'll get the rest."

"You deviant little slut," I tell her and finish off the cigarette and fight the urge to readjust now that my cock's so hard, it's being strangled by my pants.

"Eight o'clock," she says and turns away. "Do not be late. Sister hates tardiness."

She and I have one thing in common—we are devotees to every minute of every hour.

Darkland may be one of the wealthiest islands in the island chain, but it also loves to deal in another currency—*gossip*.

And the gossip in court is that Giselle and Holt—eldest and second eldest Remaldi siblings—are either trying to fuck each other or kill each other.

Really I think it could go either way.

When I enter the starboard dining hall, I find Giselle at the head of the family table, a goblet of brandy in her hand. She's wearing a gold dress stitched in crystals that glimmer in the light. Giant Summerland diamonds hang from her ears and more hang around her neck.

Giselle is the type of woman who is made beautiful by her wealth. I think if she were born in the Umbrage under the smoke and ash of the factories, her nose would appear just a little too big for her face and her eyes too close together.

"Roc," she says and smiles at me.

Because I'm a dutiful asshole, I greet her with a kiss on her bare knuckles and she blushes beneath the attention.

Two nights ago, I shot a rope of cum on her face.

She wasn't blushing then.

"Your Majesty," I say to her. "You look ravishing tonight."

"As do you. I see you're wearing the gift I bought you."

The gift is a three-piece suit tailored specifically for me. It's the same dark shade as the Remaldi velvet but made of mohair. It hides most of my tattoos save for the crocodile mouth and sharp teeth that half wrap around my throat and the ink on my hands.

"It looks divine," she says.

"Thanks to you."

She demurs.

"Sit," she orders and gestures to the chair on her left. Holt usually sits there. I see tonight she's chosen violence.

I sit.

She flicks a finger and one of the servants brings me a tumbler of Summerland whisky. It's one of the sweeter blends and tastes like caramel and spice.

"Is it too early to talk business?" she asks.

"Is it ever with you?"

The laughter that bubbles out of her throat is not amused. "Not when the future of my island is at stake. But you know that."

"Of course."

The rest of the family files in. Holt comes to a jarring halt when he sees me in his chair. His jaw flexes. I smile innocently at him.

I have not fucked Holt. Holt hates my fucking guts.

Sometimes I fantasize about liberating him from his.

Giselle holds his gaze for a second too long and then he sits in the chair on her right.

Holt is just one year younger than Giselle, but he thinks he's the one in charge because he's a man.

Clearly Holt knows nothing about the might of women.

Amara takes the chair beside me and leans in close. "You look so fucking hot in that suit."

"I know."

On the other side of the table, the two youngest cousins of the family share a laugh. There's Julia, whose parents are dead. And Matthieu whose parents are not.

Julia is destined to be married off to one of the Darkland viscounts. I actually like Julia. We play chess when the mood strikes. She's spectacularly bad at it but I let her win.

The servants bring out the first course—toasted bread with cheese and slivered roasted vegetables drizzled in balsamic vinaigrette.

"Have you decided how you'll approach your brother?" Giselle asks as she cuts into the bread with a knife. The bread cracks, then crunches beneath the blade.

"It's best if I approach him alone." I drain my whisky and gesture for another.

"You think we're just going to let you wander off on Neverland without us?" Holt asks. "So you can warn Vane? And Peter Pan? Absolutely not."

"Come on, Holt." Amara is talking with her hands, waving her silverware around. "Roc has been with us longer than he was with his brother. He no longer holds allegiance to Vane."

Giselle is watching me.

I drain the second whisky the servant brought over.

If anyone can spot my lies, I think it would be her.

"Time means nothing to blood," Holt says.

"Time means everything, Holt," I counter.

Speaking of which...

I check my pocket watch.

I have an hour and three.

We're only on the first fucking course.

"Once we've visited the fae queen to find out what we're dealing with, I suggest you all stay in Darlington

Port," I tell them. "Do not wear your royal crests. Stay inconspicuous. Don't flaunt your wealth. And for the love of god, do not provoke Peter Pan or the Lost Boys. When the time is right, I'll call for you."

"How about instead you bring Vane to us?" Holt fingers the giant rock hanging from his neck. It's about the only remaining magic in the Remaldi family, and it's both Holt's line of defense and his last hope.

The Darkland Life Shadow has been misplaced for centuries. And magic has been waning with the Death Shadow off-island.

They're getting desperate.

Of course the magical rock will work against my vicious little brother who possesses one of the most powerful entities in the Seven Isles. I'm sure it'll be *fine*.

"I'll see what I can do," I tell Holt but I won't.

The second course comes out. It's a thick red soup.

Now I'm hungry for something else.

By the third course, I can literally hear the seconds ticking down in my head.

I need to get the fuck out of here.

I check my watch again.

"Have somewhere to be?" Giselle asks.

"You know I like to meditate at a certain time every day."

"Meditate." Holt snorts as he saws into his steak.

Almost everyone in Darkland knows me as The Crocodile, the Devourer of Men.

But they don't know why.

They don't know what happens when the seconds run out.

"Eat," Holt orders. "You wouldn't want all this food to go to waste, would you, Crocodile?"

"Of course not." I give him a tight smile.

When the plates are cleared again, dessert comes out last.

"I'll skip the last course tonight," I tell them and shove back my chair.

"Oh must you?" Giselle pouts.

"I must."

"I think you should stay," Holt says.

Technically anyone beneath the dominion of the royal family has to follow a direct order.

Holt isn't stupid. It was more a suggestion than an order to test me, but not risk his limbs.

"I really must go," I counter. "But I appreciate the hospitality as always."

My skin crawls as I hunch over Giselle and kiss the back of her hand again. "Goodnight, Your Majesty."

"Goodnight, Crocodile."

She has that look on her face—a promise that I'll see her later.

Not tonight. Not if I can help it.

I start for the door.

"Wait."

My stomach churns and it takes everything I have not to lose my fucking mind.

I turn back to the dining hall.

Holt says, "We'll be on the island soon. I'll expect you to be ready to disembark."

"Of course, Your Highness."

I need to get the fuck out of here or I'm eating Holt for dinner.

"You're dismissed," he says and I bow to the room and push through the swinging door.

I have my watch in hand as I barrel down the hallway,

then use the railing on the stairwell to slide down to the lower decks.

I find a servant girl and take her hand. “Come with me,” I tell her and she tries to object but there is no *try* with me.

The clock ticks louder in my head.

Sweat breaks out along the back of my neck.

Too close.

Too fucking close.

I yank the girl into my cabin and slam and lock the door behind us.

“My lord,” she says and wrings her hands.

They all know my reputation. But I don’t need to fuck.

I need to eat.

“Apologies, little girl,” I tell her as the shift hammers behind my eyes and I catch sight of my glowing irises in the mirror over the desk.

The girl gasps, lower lip trembling.

“This will only take a moment.”

And then I wrap my hand around the back of her neck and drag her to me.

1

PETER PAN

How long until the sun rises?

The thought comes to me as we follow the Neverland road back to the treehouse, drenched in blood, steeped in victory and covered in darkness.

It is an old thought that still causes a thread of panic to travel its way up my spine and seize me by the ribcage.

Because if I am caught in the sunlight, I will turn to ash.

It takes me a few seconds to realize that I no longer have to worry about the light.

I have my shadow.

Neverland is mine again and I am hers.

The twins surge ahead on the path, but Vane is by my side. I can feel his questions hanging between us.

"What is it?" I ask, keeping my gaze on the twins. They're cajoling one another despite the fact that we're returning from a battle with their sister, the fae queen. One where she clearly drew the lines for them and they clearly chose a side—*mine.*

We will have to face the queen again and if I get my way, she'll be usurped and the twins will be crowned kings of the fae court and everything will be as it should be.

That is my preferred outcome—that I will return to what I was and Neverland will be at peace.

Captain Hook is still a wild card though and I don't like card games.

He'll have to be dealt with eventually. Cherry too.

But I'm getting ahead of myself.

"How do you feel?" Vane asks. He's no longer looking at me but I can still feel the weight of his attention.

"I..."

How do you sum up being whole again? How do you sum up the feeling of being alive where once you were dead? Maybe not literally, but spiritually, magically? I was a walking, talking man missing a soul.

How do I feel?

I thought once I had my shadow, I would return to whatever version of myself existed when I lost it. But that's impossible. I realize that now.

I am changed.

Peter Pan, the infamous Never King, has been transformed by a Darling girl, a Dark One, and two fae princes.

How do I feel?

It's an impossible question to answer.

"I'm fine," I tell Vane and he scoffs so I amend. "I'm looking forward to returning to our Darling girl," I add. "She will be screaming my name by sunrise."

I glance over at him. I have the side of him with his good eye, but I still can't tell what he's thinking. "Will you fuck her too? Fill her up so I can watch the pleasure on her face."

I'm already hard just thinking about it.

I can't remember the last time I fucked with my shadow intact. How many centuries has it been? Too many. So many I've lost count.

But a pinch of discomfort appears in the fine lines around Vane's eye. "I still have to give her pain to give her pleasure."

The twins laugh and then Bash roughly wraps his arm around Kas's neck and yanks him into his side.

"Darling knows what the cost is," I tell Vane.

"Yes, but what is *my* cost? Have you considered that?"

"No, I haven't," I admit, because there's no sense lying about it. "Tell me then."

"When she bleeds...it's not the shadow..." He curses and then pulls a cigarette from the steel case in his pocket. There's pirate blood crusted around his fingernails and dried in the grooves of his first knuckles. More of it is splattered across his face.

I like Vane the most when he is covered in carnage. It reminds me that I am not alone in my thirst for destruction.

I wait for him to light the cigarette and fill his lungs with smoke.

"Go on," I tell him.

"The shadow doesn't care if Darling girls bleed," he says. "But what I am beyond the shadow...*that does*."

I have a flash of The Crocodile lapping up Hook's blood after we cut off his hand.

Roc reveled in it.

I thought it was just a weird quirk. That fucker is insane as far as I'm concerned. I never questioned it and Hook lost his fucking mind, so I guess the act did its part.

The Seven Isles are home to so many creatures, so much

magic, so many myths and legends, that it's impossible to guess at what Vane might be. But now I have to wonder if it runs in the family.

There may be numerous monsters in the Isles, but those that thirst for blood...those are not so numerous.

Vane takes a long drag from the cigarette.

Beyond the trail, the wolves prowl in the late darkness.

As the road curves south toward the treehouse, I snap my fingers at Vane and he hands off the cigarette so I can take a hit, hold it in.

The smoke doesn't burn like it used to and I'm surprised to find I'm disappointed.

"So what are you saying?" I ask him after I've exhaled.

"I don't know."

"I think you do know but you don't want to tell me."

He sighs. "To Winnie, I am a blade and a predator with sharp teeth. If I don't cut her as one, I will tear through her as the other and I don't know what the fuck to do about that."

Hearing him call her by her name is an odd thing. An *intimate* thing. I have to push aside the flare of jealousy that they might be closer than I realized. Because of course they will be. It's inevitable. I am a king. I will always be held at arm's length. And the twins will never be closer to anyone than they are to each other.

It was always meant to be Vane.

We will all have her, but Vane might get a part of her that the rest of us can never see.

I have to be okay with that. I *am* okay with it. But it means I need to hold them both together, because without one, I will lose the other and without both...

The wolves come closer and I spot one darting through the underbrush on my left.

"So what you're telling me is, giving up the Darkland shadow will not solve your problems, so really what we should do is find you the Neverland Dark—"

"Motherfucker," he says, but there's a ring of laughter on the edge of his voice. He steals the cigarette back.

"Listen," I say, "I know what it feels like to try to grapple with being two sides of a bad coin. If there is anyone who understands it, it's me. So just fucking talk to me."

The hair lifts along my arms as the twins slow up ahead and a wolf peers out from the woods.

I am connected to Neverland once again, but it's been so long, I don't recognize the syllables of the land's language, the sharp edges of the constants, the softness of the vowels. I have to learn it all over again.

What is that gnawing in the back of my head? The feeling that something is wrong?

I look over at Vane.

Perhaps I've pushed him too far. Maybe his dark shadow is chafing against mine.

We have never been side by side in this way, two shadows of different lands.

It annoys me that I didn't consider this.

It terrifies me that it might turn out to be a problem.

"Do you feel that?" I ask.

He nods at me, his violet eye going black.

The wolf trots out to the middle of the path in front of the twins.

Vane and I slowly make our way forward, flanking the princes so that we face the wolf in a formidable line.

"This is unusual," Kas says, keeping his voice low and even. The wind shifts and his hair billows in front of his face but he doesn't make a move to fix it.

A very, very long time ago, I would run with the wolves, but the memory is so old it's more smoke than fire, barely there at all.

I haven't seen the wolves this close since I lost my shadow.

Bash whistles at him and then says, "Whatchya doing, boy?"

The wolf dips his head. Even hunched, he's still about half as tall as the twins. His coat is like a dark twilight sky—mostly black with flecks of white and gray.

He looks at us with vivid blue eyes.

"What do we do?" Kas asks.

The wolf is standing between us and the treehouse.

I am impatient to return to my Darling.

I step forward.

That feeling that something is wrong grows.

"Go on," I tell the wolf. "Back to the woods."

He straightens his shoulders and lifts his head, pulls back his lips to show gleaming sharp teeth.

"Go on. I won't tell you again."

I take another step and he turns around and runs.

But he doesn't go to the woods.

Instead, he follows the road straight to the treehouse.

2

PETER PAN

I CAN SENSE THE WOLF'S DESTINATION IMMEDIATELY.

At my side, Bash says, "Maybe we should—"

But I'm not listening and I'm sure as fuck not waiting.

I bend my knees and push off Neverland earth with all the urgency of a mortal jet plane.

I take to the air in less than a second and I'm breaking the sound barrier not long after that.

The trees rattle beneath the force of my flight.

There's no time to revel in being midair again.

Panic has my heart thudding in my ears and the blood rushing through my veins.

The wolf is after the house.

I am after the wolf.

When I land outside the treehouse, I find the front door shredded, nothing but splinters, and bile races up my throat.

"Darling!"

I shove what remains of the front door in and it bangs against the wall.

Wet paw prints cross the foyer and disappear up the stairs.

“Darling!”

Some of the Lost Boys shuffle from their rooms scrubbing at their eyes.

"Pan, what is it?" one of them asks.

“Darling!” I shout again and don’t bother with the stairs.

I hear a yelp from the loft, then a growl, and the parakeets take flight from the tree in a rolling wave.

When I land outside Darling’s bedroom, I smell the muskiness of the wolf’s pelt.

A female voice is quivering with fear from the inside.

I slam the door in and find Cherry cowering in the corner of the room and the wolf standing on the end of Darling’s bed snarling at me.

Darling is tucked on her side beneath the thin sheet, fast asleep.

I edge closer. The wolf lets out a warning growl.

I may not speak the same language—*yet*—but I know he can sense intention, especially mine. If it comes down to the wolf or Darling, I know what my choice will be.

He needs to know it too.

A warning is a warning.

“Out,” I tell him.

But he gives me one more snarl and then turns a circle on the bed and curls into Darling’s side, his eyes open and trained on me, daring me to come nearer.

What the fuck is going on?

“Cherry,” I say.

She lets out a strangled little cry. She's shaking like a leaf.

"Cherry, are you all right?"

She gulps down a breath and then wipes at her nose. "I'm fine. I'm okay. I'm—" But her eyes are bloodshot, and it gives me reason to wonder if she's been crying much longer than the last few minutes.

Everything is wrong.

Nothing feels right.

But I can't be sure it isn't the shadow realigning itself and muddying my intuition.

"Is Darling okay?" I ask next.

Cherry audibly swallows and uses the wall to bring herself upright. "She's...I..."

Vane barrels into the room behind me and rushes to the bed, but the wolf issues another rumble from his chest and Vane comes to a stop.

"What the fuck is going on?" he asks. "Why is the wolf in Winnie's bed?"

"I don't know," I answer. "You have as much information as I do."

He gives me a look like I'm being an asshole. "Okay, then why is she sleeping in her bed? I specifically told her to go to your tomb. Cherry, why the *fuck* is she sleeping in her bed?"

Cherry's eyes glaze over again and she shakes her head, lower lip trembling.

"Cherry!" Vane shouts.

"I don't know!" she yells back and then closes her eyes, purging more tears.

"Hey," I tell him. "Go have a drink."

He scowls at me and his eyes go black again. "Something is wrong."

His shadow's voice vibrates in his throat and the wolf lifts his head in interest.

I grab Vane by the shoulder. He will no longer be a match for me so I have no fear of his retaliation. And what a fucking liberation.

"Go have a drink. *Now*."

He gives me one more icy look, black eyes glinting, before shoving through the twins who are hovering by the door.

"Well this is unexpected." Bash edges around me. The wolf rests his head on his massive front paws.

"Careful, brother," Kas says.

"I know what I'm doing," Bash argues.

"You say that now but must I remind you—"

"No you must not," Bash says.

"—of the time you tried wrestling with a wolf and the wolf tried eating your stupid fucking face?"

"It's okay, boy." Bash takes another step. I'm having a hard time deciding who should get my attention—Winnie or the wolf.

How the hell is she still sleeping with all this commotion?

Bash gets a foot away from the bed and holds out his hand so the wolf can smell him. "See?" Bash says. "I'm one of the good ones."

Kas snorts.

When the wolf seems satisfied with the prince, Bash pats the wolf's head and then gives him a scratch behind the ear.

"Friends?" Bash brings his other hand around to scrub at the wolf's ruff.

Cherry tries to use our distraction with the animal as a

means to duck out of the room, but I snatch her by the wrist and wrench her back.

"Ahhhhhhh," she breathes out as my grip tightens around her arm.

"Why is Winnie in her bed and not in my tomb?" I ask her.

She swallows. Licks her lips, flutters her eyelashes. She's having a hard time catching her breath. "Maybe because she was tired."

I narrow my eyes and feel a swell of something old and familiar.

It's that same knowing feeling gnawing in the back of my head.

Cherry is lying.

But why would she lie about something like this?

I look past the twins to Darling again, her chest rising and falling with even breaths.

Something is different about the energy in the room and I can't tell if it's the wolf, my shadow, or the twins gleeful excitement.

"Is Darling okay?" I ask again and then soften my voice. "Tell me, Cherry."

Her shoulders rock with a shiver.

She and I look down at her arms at the same time and I notice she's peppered in bruises and scrapes.

"Where did these come from?"

"A parakeet got trapped in my room."

Another lie.

"*Cherry—*"

"Pan," Bash says.

"What?" I snap.

When I turn to him, I find Darling curling an arm around the wolf's neck. She nuzzles into him and breathes in deep. "I'm okay," she answers, but her voice is faraway and sleepy.

Some of my panic ebbs out.

To Cherry, I say, "Stay in the house until I need you. Understood?"

"Of course," she answers and when I drop her arm, she is gone in an instant.

The twins step back so I can go to the bedside. The wolf seems fine with me approaching now. "Are you awake, Darling?" I ask.

She looks the same. The same coarse, dark hair. The same swell of red lips, the same fan of dark lashes over pale skin.

She looks the same but she does not feel the same but the wolf is making it hard to figure out why.

His energy is everywhere, his wildness permeating the air.

"Darling?" I try again when she doesn't answer.

"Hmmm?"

"You promise you're all right?"

She breathes in the wolf's smell and seems completely unaware that she's snuggled into his side.

"I promise."

I want to rouse her. I want to hold her. I want to tell her I got my shadow back and see the excitement play across her face.

But she is so content.

For now, that must be enough.

"Come find me when you wake," I tell her.

"Okay."

She settles back into sleep.

I look over at the wolf, his head turned toward me, blue

eyes on me. “She’s mine. Do you understand me, wolf? *Mine.*”

He growls in this throat, but lets it fade out before settling his head again.

Beyond Darling’s room, the sky is turning pale blue with the rising sun.

“Stay by her side,” I tell the twins. “Call for me if anything changes and I will be here.”

The twins give me a nod before Bash settles into the wingback and Kas pulls himself up onto the windowsill.

Satisfied that Darling has a new protector, it would seem, and two fae princes to look over her, I leave her bedroom and head out into the wet morning air.

3

KAS

When my brother and I were young, our father captured a wolf cub and gave it to us as a solstice gift. We named the wolf Balder after one of our fae gods.

The wolf cub grew up to be a ferocious beast who would terrorize the court any chance he got. Eventually Father made us keep him kenneled in the stables. But Balder had slept with us every night from the moment he came home and so all alone in the stables, he would howl long into the night.

"Can someone shut up that dog?" Mother had said. "I told your father it was a horrible idea to bring that beast home."

Mother hated anything she couldn't boss around.

To keep Balder quiet, Bash and I would sleep with him in the stables, nestled amongst the dry sweet grass that lined the dirt floor.

Bash and I didn't mind it so much. No one bothered us in the stables. No one watched us and judged us and told us what we were doing wrong or what we weren't doing that we should be doing right.

And then one night, we woke up and found Balder gone and Mother standing over us. It was the middle of the night so all we could see was the golden glow of her wings and the dark silhouette of the rest of her.

"Enough of this playing in the dirt," she'd said. "You are princes and you should act the part."

"Where's our wolf?" Bash had asked.

"He ran away," Mother said and then started for the open stable doors. "I'll expect you dressed and at the gathering hall by sunup."

Except Bash and I ignored the order and scoured the woods calling Balder's name.

We eventually found ourselves at the edge of the woods where the sandy beach of the lagoon took over.

Peter Pan was at the shore staring out at the swirl of light.

He had already lost his shadow by that point, but Mother had still given us the warnings about him.

In fact, being in his territory was already a bad idea, let alone crossing paths with him.

"You can come out," he'd called, his back still to us. "I can hear you breathing."

Bash and I shared a look. Did we dare?

We had always been fascinated by Peter Pan. He was older than anyone could remember. More myth and god than man. Even Father was afraid of him and Father feared no one.

Bash was the first to step from the cover of the trees. "We're looking for our wolf," he'd said. "Have you seen him?"

"How is your mother?" Pan had asked instead.

I followed my brother out and the sand squished between my toes.

We knew there was history between Tinkerbell and Peter Pan, but the fae court had always been more gossip than fact. We weren't sure what the actual story was. We knew that when Peter Pan's name was brought up, her wings would glow brighter but her mouth would screw up into a scowl.

Tinkerbell loved and hated Peter Pan. She tried to hide the love now that she was married to the fae king.

But her wings never lied.

"Mother is well," I'd answered.

"Is she? She trying to control your lives like she did mine?" He glanced at us over his shoulder.

I think he already knew the answer, but while Bash and I weren't close with Mother, we weren't going to talk ill about her. Nani had taught us better than that.

"Your wolf is dead," he said. "I suspect Tinkerbell will know something about that." Then he turned around and stalked off into the woods.

Bash and I shared a look.

"The fuck was that all about?" Bash asked.

"Fuck if I know."

But then a swirl of light shot up from the lagoon. And there, sinking to the bottom, was our dead wolf.

Bash lights a cigarette and takes a long draw on it before handing it off to me. The treehouse is quiet, but with the early hour, I would expect nothing else.

"Now that Pan has his shadow back," Bash says, "I think we could take the court if we wanted it. Tilly may be determined to scheme and oust Peter Pan, but all of it is at the expense of her army."

There's a piece of ash hanging on the end of the cigarette. I turn it around and blow across it and the embers flare, the ash flaking off. "I noticed."

"Do we want it back? The court?"

I draw on the cigarette and hold the smoke in my lungs. "Do you?"

He rests his head against the flared side of the wingback chair. His gaze is trained on Darling. "It's all I've wanted for a very long time." He sighs and scrubs at his eyes. "But now I'm not so sure."

"I never hungered for the power that the monarchy allowed, but you know what I do miss?" I hand him back the cigarette. "The rituals. The ceremonies. The solstice celebrations. The smell of feasts and the constant beat of music filling the halls."

He smiles and nods and in an instant, Darling's room is overtaken by an illusion that is a perfect replica of our memories.

It's the dining hall at the fae palace, metal lanterns hanging from the ceiling glowing with fae magic. The smell of roasted meat and sweet cakes and herbed potatoes and honey biscuits.

It's almost painful to look at but I can't help but linger in the memory.

I hated every part of fae court life when I was a crowned prince living it.

It is a mortal sentiment, taking things for granted, missing something that is lost, but I understand it more than ever.

Everything is forever on Neverland but all of it is so easily lost.

I'm so old I've lost count.

Peter Pan is so old no one remembers when he first appeared.

And yet we still hunger for permanence and substance, something solid beneath our feet that we can call our own.

Something we can belong to.

The word *love* comes to mind.

To love and be loved.

To cling to something, not because you are afraid, but because you are happy.

Bash exhales smoke and stubs the cigarette into a nearby clay pot. "Do you know who that wolf reminds me of?" He nods at the furry black creature curled up next to Darling.

"Balder," I say easily.

The wolf's ears perk up and he opens his eyes and looks right at us.

Bash and I share a glance.

"Balder?" Bash repeats and the wolf lifts his head. Bash is on his feet in a second edging toward the bed. "Is that you, boy?"

The wolf groans and his tail thumps loudly against the mattress.

"How is that possible?" Bash scratches at the back of his head. "Balder has been dead for...a long time."

I can hear Nani in the back of my head and I repeat her words out loud to my brother. "'The lagoon gives and it takes.'"

He frowns at me.

"Father knew it too. It's why he went into the waters in the first place."

"So the lagoon gives us Balder years and years after Tink killed him? Why?"

I shake my head. "I don't think he's here for us. You remember what Nani used to say about wolves."

"Symbols of protection and strength."

"It makes sense. Of course Darling should be shielded from us. We treat her like our whore and the island is telling us to stop being pricks or the wolf will bite off our dicks."

"Don't be an idiot. Darling likes being treated like a whore. And the island shouldn't shame her for it."

He's right. For whatever reason, Darling does like what she likes and who are we to deny her?

But I can tell by the look on his face that he's having the same thought that I am.

"You know what else ended up in the lagoon," he says, his voice a rasp.

"Don't even go there," I tell him. "I don't even want to think about it."

A chill crawls up my spine.

Then Darling stretches beneath the sheet and issues a yawn. And when she opens her eyes and sees the wolf beside her, she lets out a startled yelp.

4

WINNIE

There is a massive wolf lying on the bed beside me. Heat radiates off of him. He turns his head to me, peers at me with bright blue eyes.

Kas and Bash are beside me in an instant. "It's all right," Kas says. "Apparently he likes you. Came straight to your bed this morning and wouldn't leave your side."

I instantly feel a connection to the wolf. And I swear he says to me, *It's going to be all right.*

I rub the sleep from my eyes and try to shake the fogginess from my brain.

Am I still dreaming?

In fact...

"Did you two bring me to bed?" I ask the twins.

They shake their heads. "You don't remember?" Bash asks.

"Not entirely. I remember the pirates and Vane and Cherry and then..."

Why can't I remember anything after that? I've been

blackout drunk before, I'm almost certain I didn't drink after the pirates.

Cherry asked for my help, but after that, everything is a muddy blur.

"Wait," I say. "Did Pan get his shadow?"

The twins grin.

"He did." I breathe out with a sigh of relief. "Thank god. Where is he?" I throw the sheet back and set my bare feet to the floor.

"I suspect he went out to greet the sunlight," Kas says.

"And Vane?" I ask.

Bash rolls his eyes and picks at a torn fingernail. "Brooding as usual. As if he has anything to brood about."

He says this dismissively, but I get the distinct sense there is more he's left out.

I go to him, or *no*...that's not it, exactly. I feel pulled to him. I feel like I need to...reassure him?

I can *feel* him.

Which is odd.

It's this distant hum of energy not unlike the hum I'd feel when Mom and I lived beneath a major power line in Wisconsin.

There's still blood smattered across Bash's face, red blood and blood that glitters like fish scales. I remember their sister using us as hostages.

I sense the twins' hurt but they won't speak of it and it's weird to sense it, isn't it? Or is this some new dynamic between us? Some kind of empathetic power now that the Never King has his shadow back?

I don't know what Neverland is supposed to feel like with the Never King whole again.

I reach up on tiptoes and wrap my arms around Bash's neck. "I'm sorry your sister did that to you," I tell him.

He's stiff for a second before he melts into the embrace and breathes out, his shoulders drooping.

And then I go to Kas and hug him too. He doesn't shy away from the affection and his hair slides around us, tickling my arms. "It's all right, Darling," he says. "We'll be all right."

I pull away and take his gorgeous face in my hands. His dark brow is furrowed over his bright, golden eyes. "I know you'll be all right but I know what it is to be betrayed by those who love you."

He nods.

I catch the barest shift in their demeanors. Just a sliver of the hurt ebbing out.

We still have work to do for the twins and the fae court, but first...

"Where is the Never King? Is he different with his shadow? I want to see."

"Just as domineering as ever," Bash says with a grunt. "I'd check the beach."

I make my way to the hall but stop in the bedroom doorway. "Will you make us pancakes? To celebrate?" My stomach growls at the mention of food. I'm starving and even better, I have an appetite. "I'll go fetch the Never King while you go pick cloudberries? Sound good?"

The twins look at one another and I hear the distant chiming of bells.

"I'll take that as a yes," I say and then head into the hall.

I had intended to go to Pan alone, but I hear the distant clicking of wolf nails on the hardwood floor as I leave.

The loft is empty when I come out, but the birds are chirping loudly in the Never Tree.

"Good morning," I tell them and several take flight from the branches and follow me in a swirl of feathers and a flap of wings.

The wolf comes up alongside me.

I've never had a pet. Well...scratch that. I did have a stray cat at one of our apartments years ago. I fed it dollar store tuna fish straight out of the can. He stuck around for a few months until winter set in and then I never saw him again.

I sure as hell never had a wolf.

"Why are you following me?" I ask him as I open the doors that lead to the balcony.

I don't expect the wolf to answer me, but somehow, I sense his response.

Protection.

I stop and look down at him. He cranes his neck to meet my gaze.

"Did you just talk to me?"

His long, bushy tail wags behind him.

"This is the strangest morning I've had yet in Neverland and I was once chained to a bed."

I go down the steps and the wolf follows and then he keeps following me as I cross the backyard.

We stop at the end of the dirt path when I spot Peter Pan on the sandy shoreline facing the ocean where the sun is just starting to cast a ribbon of fire on the horizon line.

I look down at the wolf. "Time to go," I tell him.

No, he says back.

"I'm talking to a wolf," I mutter. "Maybe I'm dead." Then, "If you're here for protection, I am no safer with you than I am with Peter Pan."

The wolf blinks up at me.

"Go on," I tell him again. "I need this moment alone with him."

And then we both turn our attention to Pan, to the line of his back against the glowing ocean waves.

Fine. The wolf trots off into the underbrush and I go down to the shoreline.

When I come around to stand between Pan and the lapping ocean waves, I find his eyes closed, his arms around his knees. "Sit," he orders me.

There is a faint spark of something in the center of my chest that feels like a knowing that should have a name, but doesn't.

Like I've walked into a city I've never visited but yet somehow know where all the roads lead.

"He's hovering," Pan says, his eyes still closed. "I can feel him everywhere, even on you."

It takes me a second to realize he means the wolf.

In the line of ferns and palm fronds on the edge of the beach, there is a flash of black fur.

"He said he'd give us some privacy."

Pan peeks at me with one eye. "You're talking to wolves now, are you?"

I shrug. "It would seem so."

"Sit, Darling."

I cross my legs and sit. He's warm beside me, just like the wolf, and there is a new energy surrounding him that I swear I can feel vibrating on my skin.

Everything is buzzing and for some reason, I feel like I'm not entirely in my own skin.

"You got your shadow," I say.

"I did."

"And how do you feel?"

A breath escapes him through his nose and then he bows his head. "I thought I would feel relief. I *do* feel relief. But..." He pops his head back up and squints at the horizon line.

"But what?"

"Once you know you can lose something, it's hard to dismiss the fear that you could lose it again."

I understand him, in a way. It wasn't that long ago that I was terrified of losing my mind.

But power is another thing. And I can't help but think about the conversation I had with Vane about the mighty oak. I had convinced myself I was the oak tree, resilient and determined, but knowing these powerful men, I realize I can barely understand the concept of power.

I am the tree with a bent and twisted trunk, trying to stretch herself to better light, so fragile that in every storm, her boughs creak and her roots cling to the earth praying it's enough to keep her in the ground.

The bare minimum is all I know.

I have never been powerful.

I lean into Pan and hook my arm through his, rest my head on his shoulder and try to convince him that I know a thing or two about any of this. "This time will be different."

"You sound so sure."

"I am. There's no Tinkerbell now."

He tsks. "Yes but there is soon to be a Crocodile."

"I'm sure Vane can help us deal with his brother."

Pan nods.

We turn our attention to the ocean and the brightening morning sky. Shades of pink and lavender and yellow and orange burst across the thin, wispy clouds. A flock of seagulls fly past.

Somewhere nearby, I can hear a ticking.

"What's that sound?"

Pan frowns. "What do you mean?"

"Like a clock."

He gives me a suspicious look, and then leans back and digs into his pocket and produces a pocket watch without a chain. "This?"

The ticking is louder now that it has nothing to shield it. I take the timepiece and turn it over in my hand to find delicate filigree engraved on the front side and script writing on the back.

I read the back. "The Bone Society?"

Pan looks over at it. "Yes. Purported to be the inventors of time. They are the only clock makers in the Seven Isles."

"Interesting."

"Not really."

"Anything called The Bone Society is interesting. Why that name?"

"I don't know. I never cared to ask. Time means nothing to me."

I press the button at the top of the watch and the frontside pops open revealing the clockface inside.

The hands read 7:02.

"Is the time correct?"

"I wouldn't know."

"So how would you—"

"Shhh, Darling," he says and takes the watch and snaps it shut. "Look."

The first sliver of the sun breaks over the horizon and Peter Pan exhales.

I've seen hundreds of sunrises. They're all remarkable, I'll give them that, because every one is different.

But I don't care about this one.

Instead of watching the light, I watch Peter Pan.

The fine lines around his eyes tighten as he squints. His mouth breaks open, his lips wet and then a little wrinkle appears between his brows as he fills up his lungs and holds it in.

His eyes glisten.

"It's beautiful," he whispers.

"It is," I say.

He looks over at me and his gaze sinks to my mouth.

"I missed you," he admits.

"More than the sun?" I counter.

He laughs and brings my hand to his mouth and gently kisses the backside. "I've missed the light and I've missed the warmth, but both pale in comparison to you, Darling."

"You get your shadow back and now you're a romantic?" I'm teasing him, but hearing the seriousness in his voice is making my stomach swim.

There is no way to tame a man like Peter Pan and yet I feel like I've been gifted a part of him that no one else has and that might be the most profound thing I've ever possessed when I've possessed so little.

"Romantic," he says with a dismissive air. "In the light, I will treat you like a queen, but in the dark, you will be my whore."

Heat rises to my cheeks. "I'd like that."

"Oh yeah?"

"Yes. Very much."

His gaze is turning hungry, his touch on my skin more demanding and I can't help but react to him because I am always reacting to him.

Doubly so, right now, apparently. Because I can feel his growing desire. It's not just vibrating on the air, but somehow sinking into my belly and my chest and between my legs.

"I know you're enjoying your first sunrise in like *eons*, but how would you feel about returning to the dark for a little while?" I ask.

On a breath, his nostrils flare and then he's crashing into me, his mouth on mine. His kiss is devouring and his tongue darts out to meet me, then pushes in, tasting all of me.

"To have you without my shadow was a divine treat," he says against my mouth and then kisses me again, nipping at my bottom lip. "To have you with my shadow might very well undo me." He pushes me back into the sand and covers my body with his. He's hard in an instant, digging against me and I realize I'm relieved that he still wants me even though he no longer needs a Darling to save him.

I rip off his shirt and he tears off my dress. I let my hands wander over every hard ridge of his body. He is made of stone, his skin hot as the sun warms us both.

"I want to fuck you while the sun rises," he says.

"Then what are you waiting for?" I ask a little breathless.

He unzips his pants and I immediately feel the burn of his cock at my opening.

My belly swims as our kiss deepens and he thrusts inside of me.

I gasp.

"Already so wet for me, Darling," he says, sounding impressed.

He thrusts again and picks up his tempo, fucking me hard into the sand, his cock thick inside of me and then—

He stops and pulls out of me, leaving me instantly chilled and hollow.

"What's wrong?" I ask.

He wraps his arms around me and lifts me into the air.

"Oh my god! Pan!" I tighten my hold around his neck as he flies us back to the house and into the kitchen.

We burst through the doors. He walks me back into the nearest wall and lifts me up, guiding my legs around his hips. He fucks me against the wall, grunting into me with each thrust. Then he carries us away, turns into the next room, bumps into the table and sends a vase toppling to its side. Water spills off the edge.

His mouth finds mine again and our tongues slide over one another, heat and hunger and destruction in one long breath.

But then he bumps into the coffee table, spins us at the last second so when we land on the floor, it's he on his back and me impaled on his cock.

And then we look up to find Vane in one of the leather chairs, a book open in his lap, a glass of something dark in his hand.

I wiggle my hips like I mean to lift off Pan, but he catches me around the waist and keeps me on his cock. "Ah-ah," he warns.

Vane's eyes are suddenly black.

"Enjoying yourself, are you, Darling?" Vane asks, but there's a bit of sarcasm in his voice.

"I would be enjoying myself more if you joined us."

Pan lifts me just a few inches off of him, then pushes me roughly back down eliciting a squeak from my throat.

Vane sits forward. "Why weren't you in the tomb?"

"Vane," Pan says, the head of his dick swelling at my center. "I'm buried inside our Darling. Must we do this now?"

"Answer the question, Winnie Darling," Vane says.

"I can't remember," I say.

Vane stands up, grabs me by the throat and rips me off of Pan. Pan growls his frustration.

"Why did you disregard my order?" Vane's shadow rumbles in the back of his throat.

I wrap my hand around his wrist trying to get some leverage on him. I'm on my tiptoes and completely naked. I don't have much to play with here.

When Vane's dark eyes land on me, I tense up, ready for the terror, the unease, the nausea rolling in my gut.

But there is none.

And Vane's gaze narrows to slits. "Are you bleeding?" he asks and looks me up and down.

"No."

"Then how are you withstanding the terror?"

"Maybe she's learned to ignore your bullshit," Pan says behind me.

"No one *learns* to withstand me."

Pan puts his chest to my back and slowly pulls me away from Vane and replaces Vane's hand with his, his long fingers halfway around my throat.

"Just look at her for me," Pan says, his other hand kneading at my breast, rolling my nipple between his fingers.

I hiss out and squeeze my thighs together as the pain sinks to pleasure in my clit.

"Look at our Darling whore, naked and ready for us." He leaves my breast and slides his hand down my stomach, over my clit, tightening his grip on my throat when I buck beneath him. When his fingers slide down my wetness, we can all hear the proof of my arousal.

"This wet cunt is begging to be fucked."

Vane's nostrils flare and he edges closer. His eyes are still black, but there's new interest in his body. I can see the hard ridge of him in his pants.

"Shove your cock inside of her," Pan goes on, dragging the tip of his nose up the side of my neck so his next words are a warm breath on the sensitive flesh of my ear. "And when she's screaming your name, I'll shove my cock in her mouth to shut her up."

Dark desire swirls in my gut. My clit is needy and swollen now, but Pan has flattened his palm over me, caging me against him.

"Let's use her, Vane. You and me."

God I want that.

I want to be surrounded by their violence and their sin.

My inner walls clench at the thought and I get up on tip toes just to steal any bit of movement I can against Pan's hand on my pussy.

"Naughty Darling girl," he whispers in my ear and I am suddenly mindless beneath his command.

"Please, Pan," I say, eyes slipping closed.

"Please what, Darling?"

"I...I want..."

He sinks two fingers inside of me and then uses his thumb to tease my clit.

I moan, leaning into him.

When he brings his wet fingers up to my mouth and roughly coats me with my own juices, Vane's hair goes white.

"What do you say, Dark One?" Pan asks. "Let's treat our slut the way she should be treated."

Vane strips in seconds and then he's ripping me away from Pan a second later.

He whirls me around, winds an arm around my waist, and then sits us down together in one of the leather chairs so we're both facing Pan.

There is a dark hunger on Peter Pan's face as Vane hooks my legs over his knees and spreads me wide for Pan just as he shoves his thick cock inside of me.

5

PETER PAN

WATCHING DARLING GET FUCKED IS MY NEW FAVORITE THING.

Her mouth pops open as Vane shoves inside of her and fills her up, his balls sitting snuggly against her pussy.

Fuck is she a delight.

My shadow uncurls and pulses at my sternum and I am flush with power. The feeling that I can take what I want and do what I want and nothing can touch me is consuming.

I drop into the couch and take my cock in hand, easing into my own pleasure as I watch them enjoy theirs.

They are two of the most important people on this island and I need to know that Vane can handle having her.

I need to know that I can have them both in my life and not worry about one killing the other.

The fact that Darling could ignore the Death Shadow's terror is a good sign.

The best outcome.

Darling moans as Vane punishes her pussy, the thick

underside of his shaft thrusting into her, soaking wet with her pleasure. His fingers are creating divots in the flesh of her hips, he's gripping her so hard, shoving her down on him.

She's spread wide for me so I can watch.

He knows what I like.

Darling bouncing on his cock might rival renaissance art in its beauty.

My dick is throbbing in my hand, pre-cum glistening at the slit.

Pressure is building in my head turning me fucking mindless for release.

"Oh fuck, Vane," she says, her voice high-pitched and thin.

I cross the room. Vane winds a chunk of Darling's hair around his fist and yanks her head back.

"Take him, Win. Make the king come down your throat."

She pops her lips open for me, so fucking eager.

I push inside of her wet mouth. Her cheeks hollow around me.

"Fucking hell, Darling," I say.

Vane tightens his hold on her hair and uses it to drive her up and down on me as she balances her hands on his thighs.

She chokes.

I keep going.

She moans around me and then slides her fingers over her clit.

Vane lets go of her hair to capture both her wrists behind her back.

She makes an adorable little frown as she bobs on my cock.

"Not your turn, Darling," I tell her as the pressure comes to a head. "You only get to come when we tell you to come."

Which won't be long at all.

I can't hold out.

I don't want to.

The building in my gut and the pressure in my cock is too much to bear.

I thrust deeper and spill down her throat with a loud groan.

Tears spill over her eyelids as she gazes up at me.

Another spurt and my cock throbs on the flat of her tongue.

My shadow writhes beneath my skin, satisfied and spent.

When I pull out of her mouth, I take her by the chin. "Let me see, Darling."

She sticks out her tongue. There's just a slight sheen of cum there. She swallowed the rest. "Good girl."

"I know what I'm doing," she says as the tears stream down her face. I wipe one of them away and then sink to the floor.

"Now be a good girl and come sit on my face."

6

WINNIE

VANE LIFTS ME OFF OF HIM AND CLIMBS TO HIS FEET, GUIDING ME over to Peter Pan.

"On your knees, Win," Vane commands.

I position my knees on either side of Pan's head and I can't help but clench up, sensing him below my most sensitive area.

Vane stands in front of me. He's going to make me chase down Pan's cum with his.

"Open up, Darling," he says, echoing the same words he used not that long ago, when he spit in my mouth and told me I would have no more of him.

Now look at us.

I dutifully open my mouth and stick out my tongue and he slides his cock into me, filling me up.

It's much harder to accommodate him than it is Pan, but I do my best.

It's easier when I have Pan's mouth on my pussy from

beneath me, sucking and flicking and building the pressure at my core.

Vane fucks my mouth while Pan fucks my pussy with his.

I'm so wet, I'm shocked I'm not drowning the Never King.

I moan around Vane's cock and he growls deep in his chest.

Pan sucks at my clit and I'm buzzing, electric, ready to glow for them both.

"Whatever you're doing," Vane says, "keep doing it. She's humming on my cock like a good little girl."

Pan hooks his arms around my thighs and drives me down on his face.

The groan that comes out of me practically vibrates down the length of Vane's cock.

"Just like that Win." He holds my hair back. "Don't stop."

I swirl my tongue around his shaft, then wrap my hand around the base just as Pan hits my clit again.

The orgasm takes me by surprise. One minute the pleasure is buzzing through my pussy and the next the wave is crashing over me.

I buck. Vane shoves deeper.

The pleasure pounds through me and I moan loudly until Vane sinks so deep, I choke on him. I try to pull back, to breathe, but he's in control and he's not letting up.

He fucks my mouth with another thrust, then another, and then he bursts down my throat.

I writhe on Pan's mouth as he sucks on my clit, driving the orgasm so high, I feel like I'm flying.

Vane pauses. Inhales sharply. Then spills another load on the back of my tongue.

Pan locks his arms around my thighs forcing me to stay still until he's wrenched every last ounce of pleasure from me.

"Fucking hell," Vane says on a breath. His chest is heaving and his abs are contracted, deepening the lines between each hard ridge of muscle.

There is just the barest sheen of sweat on his body and it's so fucking hot, seeing the Dark One a little disheveled and overwhelmed by me.

Hand in my hair, he slides me off of him, then paints my lips with another bead of cum. "Look at me," he orders.

He drags his thumb over the cum, then pushes back into my mouth. "Clean the rest off."

When I do, he exhales in a satisfied rush, black eyes glittering.

"Our good little Darling whore," Pan says after he slides out from beneath me. "Belly full of our cum." He wraps his arm around me, his hand just above my belly button. "Just the way we like you." Leaning over me, he plants a gentle kiss on the curve of my throat and I can't help but laugh, both at the hard and softness of these men, and the tickling breath of Pan's affection on my hot skin.

There is a flare of warmth in my chest now, and it's not from being fucked the way I like.

It's something else.

Something deeper.

These men are mine and I am theirs and—

My stomach churns. I clamp my hand over my mouth.

"Win?" Vane's brow sinks in concern. "What is it?"

Pan comes around to stand beside him. "Darling?"

"I don't...I feel a little light—"

"Goddammit," Vane says and scowls at Pan. "We overdid it. I told you we needed to be careful and—"

"She's fine," Pan says. "She just needs some food. Bash!"

"Wait," I say as the loft spins a little and I reach out for one of them.

Vane is there in an instant.

"Does anything hurt?" he asks.

I'm about to tell him no, it's just a little nausea when a searing pain shoots across my forehead.

I groan and sink into Vane's arms.

"Something is wrong," he says on a growl.

"I can fucking see that," Pan says back.

"Just...I...can..."

"Maybe she needs air," Vane suggests.

"I think I'm going to—"

Everything gets blurry. The boys are nothing but smudged shadows and there's a ringing in my head that wasn't there before and a whispering in the far dark recesses of my mind.

Let me in.

Let me in.

And then everything goes dark.

7

PETER PAN

Darling slumps and Vane scoops her up easily, cradling her against his chest.

I nudge her beneath the chin and call her name, but she's out cold.

"Something is wrong," Vane tells me, his eyes black and his voice rumbling.

"I can fucking see that."

"Where the fuck is Cherry? Something happened while we were at Hook's."

"Give her to me."

Vane's scowl deepens. "Fuck off." He turns his body, holding Darling away from me.

"Now you're being a possessive prick? Not that long ago, you were telling *her* to fuck off."

He frowns at me. "Is a man not allowed to change his mind?"

The twins' laughter wends into the loft as they enter in

through the kitchen. They're telling a story about their grandmother and her cloudberry syrup recipe.

"Boys," I call.

They come into the loft and look between all three of us still standing there naked.

Bash's mouth drops open. "You had a fuck party and didn't wait for us to come home?"

Kas comes to Darling still draped over Vane's arms and pushes the damp hair from her eyes. "What's wrong with her?"

"We don't know," Vane says. "She just passed out."

"Get her to the couch," Kas orders.

We don't typically follow the orders of banished princes, but Kas knows a thing or two about mortal ailments that he learned from his grandmother.

Vane takes Darling around to the couch and gently lays her in the corner. Kas grabs one of the pillows and tucks it beneath Darling's knees, then takes a second and puts it beneath her feet, propping her legs up.

He rests his ear to her chest.

I can hear her heart beating without the nearness. The steady thump-thump.

Her breathing is fine too.

In fact, everything I can hear and sense and see of her tells me she's fine.

"Is she sick?" Bash asks and sits on the edge of the low table in the center of the room.

"No one gets sick on Neverland." I crouch beside Darling and scan her face.

"Darling isn't technically from Neverland though," Bash points out. He has a handful of picked cloudberries and he pops one in his mouth. "Maybe we should take her to her mortal realm."

I sit beside him on the table and steal one of the berries from his hand. "She's not leaving my sight."

"Then what do you want to do?"

The longer she's unconscious, the worse I feel. I could pretend we fucked her into fainting, our fragile Darling girl. But she's not waking up.

What the fuck is happening?

Nails click on the hardwood floor and a second later, the wolf is back. He looks up at me with what is, *I swear to fucking god,* a disapproving glare.

"You can fuck off too," I tell him.

He turns away from me and hops up on the couch, nestling into Darling's side.

"Pan," Vane coaxes.

"Yes, I know." I run my hand through my hair, considering my options as new heaviness sinks in my chest. Once upon a time, before I lost my shadow, I could alter anything on Neverland. I could make things appear out of thin air.

But heal someone? Far more complicated, not as reliable, and never worth the risk.

My gut twists as the seconds tick by in my head and Darling still doesn't wake.

I could try to heal her if I knew what the fuck was wrong with her. I don't sense anything and that's the problem.

In fact...there is an odd sort of stillness to her. Even before I had my shadow, I could sense the hum of her nearness, the warmth of her presence.

And now, she's just quiet.

I hate desperation.

I hate asking for help even more.

But I'm not just going to sit on my ass and hope for the best.

Not where Darling is concerned.

I look up at Vane. “Go get Smee,” I tell him. “And hurry.”

He doesn’t argue. Doesn’t hesitate. He’s dressed and gone in seconds.

It’s hard to ignore the fast thump of his heart.

Vane is just as anxious as I am.

8

BASH

WHILE WE WAIT FOR THE DARK ONE TO RETURN WITH THE PIRATE, Peter Pan paces the loft and I busy myself in the kitchen even if our dysfunctional family breakfast is now up in the air.

Keeping my hands occupied is just the distraction I need. I've always loved being in the kitchen. It's about the only thing I inherited from my mother, though she never actually loved it.

When she was lecturing Kas and I about our duties and our roles as crowned princes of the fae court, she would remind us of where she came from and the sacrifices she made to get to where she was.

And when she would find me in the kitchen helping the staff measure and pour and stir for an upcoming dinner, she would practically pop a rib.

There may have been common fae blood in her veins, but she wanted to pretend that working with our hands was now beneath us.

Nani was queen long before Tinker Bell was and Nani worked with her hands until the day she died.

"You worried about Darling?" Kas asks as he pulls himself up on the counter behind me.

I scoop flour out of the canister. "Not really. I think if something were really wrong, Pan or Vane would know it."

"You think we're mistreating her?" he asks next.

"Oh definitely."

He snorts. "We're all depraved assholes. She's probably better off without us."

I look at my twin over my shoulder. He's still shirtless. We usually are. There's just something about feeling the sun and the Neverland ocean breeze on your bare skin that'll make you hate clothes real quick.

Plus I look better shirtless.

"Speak for yourself," I tell Kas. "I think she's better with me."

He snorts again and rolls his eyes and then tosses a cloudberry into the air, catching it with his open mouth a second later.

"You give any more thought to what we'll do if we reclaim our throne?"

I crack open an egg and the white beads through the split. "The fae has always expected the royal line to reside in court and marry and work really fucking hard at banging out an heir."

"Yep."

"I'm actually surprised our dear sister hasn't married yet."

"She always did go her own way."

It makes me wonder what she wants out of all this. She's doing what she thinks is expected of her, and yet she is shirking all of the traditional roles of a queen.

With the ingredients in the clay bowl, I grab one of the wooden spoons from the drawer and start mixing. "Can you imagine all four of us living in the fae palace with our Darling queen?"

Kas and I look at one another.

It's a ridiculous notion, my brother says in our language.

"Don't even fucking think about it," Pan says from the doorway.

There's a drink in his hand. He upends the glass and drains the liquor. "But..." he adds and breathes around the heat of the drink. "This is no royal home." His gaze goes distant. "We could build her a new one. A castle fit for a queen."

"Three kings and a Dark One?" Kas says behind me. We can all hear the sarcasm in his voice.

Now that is a ridiculous notion, I tell him.

Pan leans against the door frame, his eyes on Darling still on the couch in the next room. "I always dreamed of a united Neverland." He looks down at the empty glass in his hand and turns it this way and that, catching the sunlight. "Is that a ridiculous notion?" When he lifts his gaze again, his blue eyes are trained on us.

He understood our language that time.

Has he always?

Or is it the return of his shadow?

"No more fighting and conniving amongst ourselves?" Kas says. "It does sound like a dream."

Pan nods. "A Neverland dream. One I never wish to wake from."

Just then the front door bangs open. It creaks on its broken hinges.

I leave the pancake batter behind and my twin follows me as I follow Pan into the loft.

Vane and Smee are just coming up the stairs.

"I'm shocked he talked you into it, Smee," I say.

She's wearing a gauzy sleeveless shirt with several buttons undone from the collar exposing the odd emblem she has tattooed on her chest. Her locs are tied up on the top of her head and held back with a strip of cloth the color of firecracker flowers.

Smee ignores me and comes around the couch and kneels beside our Darling girl. Balder opens his eyes to her but clearly doesn't view her as a threat. In fact, his tail wags like he's happy to see her.

"How long has she been out?" Smee asks.

"About a half hour," Pan answers.

Smee peels back one of Darling's eyelids and checks her pupils. Then she runs her fingers over Darling's neck, then her shoulders.

"What were you doing?" she asks as she continues her check.

Darling is still naked but Pan covered her with a blanket. He's dressed again.

"Is that relevant?" Vane asks.

Smee looks over her shoulder at him as he stands, brooding, beyond the couch, arms crossed.

I'm not sure if he was more of a prick when he hated Darling or now when he's clearly falling for her.

Smee pulls a small vial from the pocket of her trousers.

"What is that?" Pan asks.

"Smelling salts," Smee answers. "Potent, safe, but effective. Do I have your permission to try it?"

Pan inhales and gives her a nod.

Smee uncorks the top and puts the vial beneath Darling's nose.

9

WINNIE

I JOLT UPRIGHT, SOMETHING SHARP FILLING MY SENSES. BESIDE ME, the wolf sits up.

"Holy shit," I gasp out and then suck in a breath. "What the hell?"

"I told you she was fine," Bash says.

Vane turns away and folds his hands at the back of his head.

I blink through some of the fog and look over at the woman crouched beside me. "Who are..." I frown. "Do I know you?"

There is something vaguely familiar about the woman, like a dream I know the shape of, but not the finer details.

"Get her some clothes," Pan says to Kas. "Vane, you go get her fresh water."

"I'm not leaving her side," Vane argues.

"I can get her water," Bash suggests.

"Vane will be faster," Pan says.

"You don't give me orders," Vane argues.

The woman leans into me. She smells like rose oil and something smoky and sweet. She takes my hand in hers. There is a crossroads of pale pink scars across her knuckles.

The boys are still arguing.

"Do you feel better?" the woman asks.

"Yeah I think so." I smooth over my hair. "Who are you?" I ask.

"Samira," she answers. "Smee," she amends.

"Hook's right-hand woman."

Did I see her at Hook's house when we confronted him and Tilly? Is that why I feel like I know her?

"Why are you here?" I ask her.

"You passed out," she says.

"Oh. And you—"

"Know a thing or two about mortal women and magic in the Isles."

"I see."

The line of her dark brow draws to a deep V. "Do you?"

"Ummm...I think so?"

Her eyes search me and heat flames in my cheeks. She was expecting me to give the right answer and I clearly didn't.

What don't I know?

"All of these powerful men," she says and lowers her voice, "blind to power when it looks them right in the fucking eyes."

"Wait, what do you—"

Pan interrupts me. "Will she be okay?"

"She's tired and malnourished," Smee answers. "Feed her more."

Pan briefly looks at me before turning back to Smee. "That's it?"

"That's it. Now, Cherry? That was the deal."

"No," Vane says. "The deal was we'd return Cherry to you. Not when."

Smee sets her hands on her hips. There's a dagger sheathed at her left side, the hilt wrapped in worn brown leather. Several runes are etched into the metal of the blade. Shapes and lines that remind me of the runes carved on my back.

She is just a few inches from the blade and could easily pull it before the others would reach her.

"When then?" she asks.

"Tomorrow," Pan answers.

"We're throwing her a party," Bash says.

"A farewell party," Kas adds.

"Let me speak to her," Smee says.

All four of the boys stare at Smee and I sense the warring of wills.

Pan finally shouts, "Cherry!"

The Lost Boys are in one of the downstairs rooms yelling and laughing at one another.

"Cherry!" Pan yells again.

"I'm coming!" Her voice rises up to the loft and then her footsteps are hurrying up the main staircase a second later.

When she reaches the landing, she comes to a halt. "Oh, Smee. Hi."

"I'm here to collect you. I would prefer you come now as would your brother."

Cherry folds her arms over her middle and looks at Vane.

"I informed Smee we're throwing you a farewell party," he says and levels her with a look.

"Right. Yes. That's right." She smiles at Smee. "And I still have some packing to do. Not a lot. Just a few things and then tomorrow I'll come..."

Everyone notices she cuts herself off before she says "home".

I don't usually feel pity for other people and I barely know Cherry, but I do understand a thing or two about wanting a place to belong.

"Jas is excited to have you back," Smee says.

"I'm excited to come back," she answers. "First thing tomorrow."

Smee examines Cherry's face for another second longer and then finally nods and turns back to the boys. "If she's not returned to Hook by tomorrow safe and sound, I'll tear out all of your eyeballs and eat them in a dipshit stew. Got it?"

Bash laughs. "Smee, you always were my favorite pirate."

She smiles tightly at him. "And you are my favorite dipshit."

He claps his hands in admiration and laughs again. "Let me walk you out."

They disappear down the main staircase.

Pan sits on the coffee table in front of me and hunches closer. "Darling?" His gaze is searching. There is a sensation curdling in my gut like I want to shrink away and hide, but I don't know why that'd be.

I will never run and hide from Peter Pan ever again.

"Yes?"

"Are you sure you're all right?" he asks.

"I'm fine. I promise. Just tired like Smee said. A lot has happened."

Kas sits at the other end of the couch. "She has a good point."

But Pan frowns at me and Vane hovers just behind him, his attention penetrating too.

"I promise you didn't break me by fucking me. Okay?" I give them a laugh to reassure them.

Then Cherry scoffs and turns away and thuds back down the stairs and the flash of an old memory darts through my head.

A memory of Cherry and...*something*.

A bird stuck in her room? Wasn't it?

Vane turns to follow Cherry, but Peter Pan stops him. "Don't, Dark One."

"She's hiding something.

"Smee said Darling is fine."

"You're going to believe a pirate? Who is our enemy?"

"Smee is not our enemy," Pan argues. "She's probably the most neutral party on this island."

Vane throws up his hands and turns away.

"Do not go to Cherry, do not touch Cherry and do not kill her," Pan warns.

Vane barely acknowledges the warning before he grumbles and leaves the room.

"He's on edge," I say to Pan.

"He always is," he jokes. "He'll be all right."

But even I can hear the doubt in Peter Pan's voice.

In fact, I have the distinct impression Vane is *this close* to snapping.

10

ROC

"I FEEL LIKE WE'RE IN THE FUCKING MIDDLE AGES," HOLT SAYS AS we make our way to the fae palace. "No cars? No transportation at all? Neverlanders just walk everywhere on foot? *Barbaric.*"

Giselle has several folds of her dress in hand, lifting the hem out of the dirt as she walks on her heeled boots.

Beside me, Amara laughs at her brother and sister. "I quite like it," she says. "Neverland is one of the last wild places in the Seven Isles. Don't you think?" She turns to me and a lock of her blond hair escapes a pin and curls over her forehead. The late morning light warms my skin and rims her in gold.

"I think anything left to be what it was instead of trying to be something it isn't should be commended."

Clasping her hands behind her back, Amara nods. "I suppose I should respect that about Peter Pan and his Neverland."

His Neverland.

I may be immortal, but even I am not as old as Peter Pan.

When I was just a child in the Darkland highlands, there were whispers even then of the man who might be a god.

Which begs the question—can he be killed? Can he die? Because if he can't, dealing with him would require finesse and creativity.

Should we come to a crossroads where Peter Pan needs to be dealt with, that is.

The fae palace finally comes into view and Holt grumbles with relief. "Finally."

"Whoa," Amara says beneath her breath.

We stop together on the foot path to take in the sight.

The fae palace is one of the most idyllic places in the Isles. Several spires dot the landscape and the stone glitters like an alabaster seashell just beyond a large, arched gate.

I am aware that most people would label the fae palace as "straight out of a storybook" but I can't help but be reminded of the myth of Hansel & Gretel and the witch's house made of candy.

That which looks magical and inviting is not always a place you want to be invited to.

When we come to the gate, two fae guards are already waiting for us. Their wings are thick and glistening dark green like algae skimmed off the bottom of a swamp. The man has horns that curl over his forehead.

The woman wears a wide-eyed startled look meant for surprise funerals and planned orgies.

"The queen is expecting us." Giselle's smile is carved from impatience.

"State your name," the man asks.

"State my name?" Giselle huffs.

"Honestly, sister," Amara says, "would you let in just anyone at the Darkland palace?"

Holt sneers at me. "We let him in."

"They let me into more than just the palace," I say back.

"My name is Giselle Remaldi, Royal Queen of Darkland, Duchess of Noir. And as mentioned, the fae queen is expecting us."

The guards look over our group. The cousins stayed on deck so it's just Giselle, Holt, Amara and I. We're all in Remaldi black.

"Weapons are to be surrendered at the gate," the woman instructs with a wobble to her demands. "You can collect them again when you leave."

"You must be joking," Holt says.

"I don't think the fae joke, Holt," I tell him.

He scowls at me. It makes his eyes disappear, his nose turn up.

I wonder what face he would make if I cut off his fingers and jammed them up his ass.

I remove the dagger in my boot and the second one attached to my belt. Amara follows my lead and takes the sword from around her waist.

Giselle gives Holt a pointed look and he mutters a string of curse words before removing his own weapons.

When the guards are satisfied, a third man who had been waiting in the watch tower, takes flight from the top deck, presumably to announce our arrival. His wings are silent as they beat at the air.

There are no fae on Darkland. There never have been. So as the fae flies off, Giselle and Holt track his flight with barely restrained awe.

"When we get inside," Holt says, "let me do the talking."

Giselle snorts. "You are not the authority here."

"You don't know how to deal with other women. You get snippy."

"I do not get snippy!"

"This is going to go swimmingly," Amara says.

I dig a handful of peanuts out of the pocket of my trousers and crack one open. Amara laughs.

"Why do you always insist on carrying those around with you?"

"They help stave off my appetite." I pop a peanut into my mouth and toss the shell.

"And which appetite would that be?" Her expression has turned devious.

"Temper your horniness, princess. Or it's bound to get you in trouble."

"I suspect the moment I met you, Roc, I was in trouble."

I crack another nut. "You aren't wrong."

The large, arched doors at the entrance to the palace clank open.

I toss another shell, then return the peanuts to my pocket as the fae queen comes out to greet us.

She is clearly trying to rival Giselle for being the most ravishing royal in a dress that hugs her curves, but doesn't take away from the beauty of her wings. Hers are a shimmering gossamer with a sensuous curve on the forewing, and a sharp turn on the hindwing.

Unlike Giselle, however, she's chosen a necklace with a single emerald pendant.

I can't help but think this was on purpose. As if to say she doesn't need to glitter with jewels to prove her significance.

It's always interesting to me to watch how women in

places of authority portray themselves, especially when faced with opposition.

Women fascinate me. They are almost always underestimated, which makes them potentially some of the most lethal opponents.

Like walking up to a jungle cat thinking you're going to give its head a gentle little pat and instead it bites off your whole goddamn arm.

That's what women in power are like.

Usually.

Sometimes they're just spoiled brats.

"Your Majesty," Giselle says and gives the fae queen a shallow bow. "How good of you to invite us here and into your home."

"I'm glad you could make it." Her wings go still and her eyes find me behind the royals.

"Crocodile." She takes a breath and her tits swell at the plunging neckline of her dress. "I'm so happy to see you."

Holt's upper lip curls.

"Likewise."

She waits, hands clasped behind her back.

I know what she's waiting for.

In current company, I'm the only non-royal here.

"Don't just stand there," Holt says. "Bow to the queen."

The fae queen lifts an eyebrow.

I know they all think that this is some kind of degradation, the royals putting the peasant in his place. But I fall easily to my knees.

The fae queen is pleased with this, as if by bowing to her, I've relinquished something. People like the queen don't realize that by giving them what they want, I take something in turn.

Pride is most everyone's greatest weakness. That and

fucking. I've watched grown men lose their minds over a hole.

I lose my mind over just two things: blood and unshelled peanuts.

Satisfied that I've done my duty of being obedient, the queen says, "Rise," and then, "Come with me."

The queen leads us to the throne room.

It's domed and partially below ground. Vines are webbed over the ceiling where lanterns hang from wrought iron chains, the insides glowing with fae magic.

Neverland is vibrant with it. Even more so than when I visited the island last.

A servant—a brownie wearing leather boots and a hat with a brim that curls like an ocean wave, pours us wine into goblets and hands them off.

Holt sniffs his but doesn't drink. He probably thinks its poisoned or hallucinogenic. I've heard the stories about faerie wine. Never stopped me from gorging myself on it.

I take a long drink to show the fae queen I half trust her. If she wants to poison me, I'm not sure why she would have gone to all this trouble of bringing me here. But if that is her plan, I guess I respect her for it.

"Your Majesty, Queen Tilly," I say, "you promised me secrets. We're all waiting with bated breath."

"Yes, of course. But first I need to know that you'll help me defeat Peter Pan."

"Defeat him?" Giselle doesn't bother to hide her incredulity.

"It can be done," the fae queen argues.

"Debatable," I say and circle the room.

"Peter Pan has no bearing on us," Holt says. "Why would we make him an enemy?"

"Because Peter Pan will defend Vane to his last breath. Which means if you want your shadow back, you'll have to deal with Pan in one way or another."

Giselle and Holt turn dour. They knew this was a possibility. Even if Vane wasn't loyal to Peter Pan, Pan would still have a hard time letting anyone come on his island and start taking power away from it.

I drain my glass and suddenly the brownie is there refilling me. I could get used to this.

"What do you propose?" Amara asks. She's hovering by her sister's side. She may be least likely to rule, but sometimes she does tend to cram her head up Giselle's ass to get on her good side.

The fae queen sets her glass down and folds her hands in front of her. I notice she didn't touch the wine.

Smart girl. Best to keep a clear head when dealing with a Crocodile.

"Peter Pan has two weaknesses," the queen says. "Vane and his Darling."

I come to a stop, a sudden chill crawling up my spine. "There's a new Darling on the island?"

The fae queen regards me with a look that feels like a secret. "Wendy's great-great granddaughter."

I am not a man that lives in the past, but hearing Wendy's name yanks me back anyway by years and years and years and makes me feel things I'd rather not feel.

She's dead now. Mortals die quickly on mortal soil after all, but even dead, she lifts the hair along the nape of my neck as if she were a ghost in the room, exhaling on my skin.

If I am endlessly fascinated by women, I was in total awe of Wendy Darling.

She is the only person to ever beat me at a game of chess.

In the beginning, I fucked around with her because I knew Peter Pan wouldn't.

But in the end, I realize she was fucking around with me because she could.

I wanted to hate her. Even more so when she denied me and told Peter Pan to take her back to her insufferable mortal land.

But eventually I came to respect her for the magic she wielded over me.

There are not many people I would allow to put a collar around my neck.

But Wendy Darling would have been an exception.

"So what do you propose?" Giselle asks. "Use the Darling in a hostage scenario?"

"Threaten Vane's life?" Holt suggests.

The cool fingers of dread claw into my heart.

I had not intended for this island visit to get messy, but if Holt so much as lays a hand on my brother, I swear to fucking god, I will cut off his hand like I did Hook's. But unlike Hook, I'll make Holt eat his. One knuckle at a fucking time.

"You won't be able to get near enough to Vane," Tilly says and some of the anxiety eases out of my shoulders. "But the Darling..."

"What's the name of this one?" I ask and keep circling the room.

"Winnie."

"She anything like Wendy?"

The queen lifts a shoulder in a half shrug. "She's feisty.

Smart, too, I suspect. She did help Peter Pan get his shadow back."

"The fuck?" Holt says. "You could have fucking told us that before we came here."

Tilly grits her teeth. I can hear her molars grinding together from clear across the room. She takes a breath and then says, "He only just now reclaimed it, which means if we are to strike against him, the only time to do so would be now, when he's still remembering how to harness the magic."

Giselle clucks her tongue. "Or we can forget about the Darling entirely and use our most potent weapon." Her greedy gaze lands on me. "This is why you hailed for the Crocodile, is it not?"

I stop when I reach the dais where the throne sits in the center.

"Roc?" Giselle asks. "Let's hear your contribution to the predicament."

Without an invitation, I step up on the dais and go to the throne. It has a sunburst at its back with vines twinning around the rays. There are insects and squirrels and other woodland creatures cast around it with the arms curved over to look like talons.

When I go around to the backside, I spot a familiar maker's mark stamped into the metal—wings with a circle in the center.

The Myth Makers.

There are several societies in the Seven Isles older than the cities and villages themselves.

The Myth Makers.

Death's Hand.

The Ancient Order of Shadows.

And my favorite, and one I happen to belong to—The Bone Society.

I wonder if the fae queen knows her throne is likely imbued with the supposed dark magic wielded by the secret society.

I could tell her.

But I probably won't.

"What is the secret?" I ask and come off the dais. "You promised me."

The queen clasps her hands behind her back. "As you know, I can get inside most mortal minds without much effort at all and up until recently, Peter Pan tasked me with using my power to root around inside a Darling's head to find the location of his shadow."

"Yes, yes. This we know." I pull a peanut out, crack it between my fingers. "Please do get on with it."

The queen narrows her eyes at me. I suppose I'm pushing her authority with my tone. Sometimes I forget to pretend to be submissive.

"Getting inside the heads of the Darlings has borne fruit," she says. "Secrets of Peter Pan's."

"Go on," Giselle says.

I pop a peanut into my mouth.

Tilly's wings shift from green to turquoise and I sense that what she's about to reveal excites her more than it should.

This better be good or I'm eating the fae queen for wasting my fucking time.

Tilly sucks in a breath and says, "Peter Pan never returned Wendy to the mortal realm."

I swallow bits of the peanut and look at the fae queen searching her face for a game.

And then the chess pieces start moving in my head.

"If Wendy was never returned, then how did the Darling line continue?"

The queen's wings buzz back and forth. "That's where it gets interesting."

I dust off peanut shell from my hands. "Show me."

"Excuse me?"

"If you can get inside a head, you can show me the memory. Don't deny it."

She clamps her mouth shut, ruby red lips thinning into a frustrated line.

I go to her. She backpedals.

"Show me."

"I can't—"

"You want this island, do you not? That's why you called me here. You need my help. You want my help, you give me proof."

I reach out for her hand. She tries to snatch hers back, but my fingers circle her wrist and drag her into me. "Show me, little girl."

She huffs, furrows her brow. The fae live long lives. I'm not entirely sure how old Tilly is, but I guarantee she isn't as old as me.

"Fine," she says and then the throne room disappears and I'm suddenly Wendy and I'm being yanked out of Peter Pan's grip.

"Don't leave me," Wendy screams. "Pan! Don't...please..."

Peter Pan pulls a blade from his side and slits a guard's throat. Blood geysers. He stabs another.

"Get him!" someone shouts.

Pan backpedals. I get further away, but my arm is outstretched and there's panic beating at my breastbone.

"Get Roc!" she yells. "Please get Roc and come back for me!"

When I stumble out of the memory, there are tears in my eyes. They aren't mine exactly. Or maybe they are.

I can still feel Wendy's panic thumping in my chest.

He left her.

He fucking left her.

And he didn't tell me even though she begged him to.

Unless...

I blink back to reality and search the queen's face.

Can the queen make up fake memories? I suppose I couldn't put it past her.

"Tell me how the Darling line continued."

"Wendy told Peter Pan she'd already had a child," Tilly explains. "So he didn't think anything of leaving her."

"I noticed." The words come out through clenched teeth.

"Wendy was lying, of course. She told him she had a child because she had wanted to stay in the Isles with you." Tilly taps at her chest. "I could feel her desire for that right here. A heaviness I still have a hard time shaking."

"Then why did she deny me?" I challenge.

"Because of what you did to Hook."

I tsk. "That was no business of hers."

"Wasn't it?"

"He deserved what he got."

Tilly cants her head. "Did he?"

"Get on with it, queen. How did the line continue if Wendy never returned?"

"Because when Wendy Darling left Neverland, she was pregnant."

I can hear all of the things the fae queen is not saying.

She left pregnant. She did not arrive pregnant. And what I am...it does not so easily procreate.

Which means...

Heat rises in my throat and for the first time in a long time, the shift threatens to overwhelm me outside of the seconds and the minutes and the hours.

Somehow, I keep it at bay.

I must amend my list. I will lose my mind over *three* things.

Blood and unshelled peanuts and revenge.

11

CHERRY

I UNCORK A BOTTLE OF WINE AND GUZZLE IT BACK.

When the alcohol settles in my stomach, I sway a little on the edge of my bed and look around my room.

I should go.

Don't even bother packing. Just slip out a side door and through the woods and find a ship I can sneak onto in Darlington Port.

The pit in my stomach is growing heavier by the second.

"Cherry?"

"Ahhh!" I jolt. The bed squeaks and I throttle the wine bottle like a weapon.

Bash frowns at me from the open doorway. "Are you okay?"

They're going to find out. If Winnie hasn't told them yet...they're going to find out and then they're going to do very bad things to me.

There is no one I can turn to.

I've always had no one but it's hitting me especially hard right now just how very alone I am.

"I'm fine," I answer. "What's up?"

It's been hours since Smee left. Bash has showered, his hair wet and slicked back save for a few strands over his forehead. He's shirtless because he always is. Sometimes I would catch myself just staring at his abs and the tattoos that run over his torso.

I might have been in love with Vane all these years, but I always felt safest with the twins.

No, maybe that's not right. I'm not sure there is such a thing as safe on Neverland.

But the twins made me feel less alone.

I can barely look Bash in the eye now.

"We're throwing you a going-away party," he says. "I'll make you one party food. Your choice. What'll it be?"

I need to leave. I take another drink from the wine.

"I have everything for lavender biscuits, the lemony ones you like." He tilts his head and scans my face. "Or the honeysuckle tarts."

I take another drink and wince.

"Cherry?"

"Honeysuckle tarts." I'm practically vibrating. I want to vomit.

Bash comes further into the room. "Are you sure you're okay?"

"Of course."

"You know, it might be for the best, you returning to Hook's territory."

I snort. "Are you kidding me?"

Bash cocks his head. "Cherry, listen—"

"My brother didn't want me in the first place. Do you know that when he left England, I snuck onto his ship because I couldn't stand the thought of being left with our father? Our father beat Jas every chance he got and sometimes when he was really angry, he'd slap me around too. But Jas never wanted me around either. When you all took Smee, he came to me and convinced me it was 'good form to make a great sacrifice for the family.' He told me trading places with Smee would only be temporary. A few weeks at most. And then when the weeks drug on and on, I realized he wasn't coming back for me so I decided to make the most of it and now look."

I run my hand beneath my wet nose. "I made this my home because it was the only option I had."

Tears spring to my eyes. I didn't mean to admit all that. Sometimes my mouth runs before my brain does.

But don't they know they left me no choice? Winnie changed everything. She is the only reason they're getting rid of me now.

I sniff and a tear streams down my face.

Bash sighs and sits on my bed beside me. Our knees bump and I am reminded of what it felt like the first night I decided to say screw it and got drunk on faerie wine and made out with Bash for the rest of the night.

He didn't fuck me even though he could have.

I would have let him.

There were nights after when he would come down to my room and climb into my bed and cast me an illusion that reminded me of the apple orchards not far from where I grew up. Every time he cast the illusion, the magic would become more accurate until it became so real, it made me sob and Bash would pull me into his side and run his fingers through my hair and just let me cry.

Kas may be the one with the bleeding heart, but Bash was the one who went out of his way to make me feel better.

More tears stream down my face and when I suck in a snotty breath, I catch the faint scent of apples.

When I look up, there is a shadow of an apple tree cast on my wall and bright pink petals are fluttering down from the ceiling.

The tears fall faster. I should have just asked Bash to help me. I should have begged him to help me stay.

I didn't have to turn on Winnie.

But they'll never forgive me now.

Why did I do that?

Bash takes my hand in his, threads our fingers together. His skin is dry and a little cold, but his grip is sure. "It's going to be all right, Cherry. You'll see."

The tears return. "Bash."

"Yes?"

"I have to tell you—"

"*Cherry*."

Vane is suddenly taking up the space of my open doorway.

"Oh right," Bash says. "I forgot to tell you, the Dark One is looking for you." He gives my hand a pat.

My stomach drops to my toes.

I could risk telling Bash. I can never tell Vane.

"Come," Vane orders.

"Where?" I look between him and Bash. Bash gives me a shrug.

"Get the fuck up right now, Cherry and come with me."

I set the wine bottle aside and rise from the bed and sway a little. Bash stays where he is.

Do they already know? Is Vane about to kill me?

I'm sure Vane can hear the loud thumping of my heart and he knows I'm terrified even though he hasn't turned his power on me.

Taking a deep breath, I follow him down the hall and out of the house.

Vane is silent for the first several minutes and I follow silently beside him as he follows the road that winds away from the house and to Darlington Port.

When he chased me not that long ago, we used the woods, not the beach.

Maybe everything is okay.

Maybe—

"Cherry," he says.

"Yes."

"Why wasn't Winnie in the tomb when we got back?"

I swallow loudly and I know he can hear that too.

There is very little I can hide from Vane.

"I already told you—"

"Don't lie to me, Cherry." He stops in the middle of the road and pulls out a cigarette, lights it with a flick of the lighter. The flame paints light across his face as the sun sets beyond the island and the inner land turns dark.

"Is something wrong?" I ask trying to prolong the inevitable, trying to think of a good way to talk myself out of this one.

I used to be good at this.

I was young when Jas left England and I snuck away with him, but I was old enough to learn a thing or two from our father.

Our father might have been an asshole in the privacy of our home, but in public, everyone loved him. He was a respected lawyer who served as chief minister to the king. And what I learned from him was that it was always better to have two sides and best to hide the one that did bad things.

"Tell me what happened," Vane asks. He takes a hit from the cigarette and squints against the smoke clouding up around his face.

It still hurts to look at him.

I know he doesn't want me, but just being near him makes my gut hurt and my chest fill with butterflies.

If I could give something, anything, to make that feeling go away, I would.

"There was a bird trapped in my room," I start and then someone flies out of the shadows and barrels into Vane and tackles him to the ground.

"Oh my god!" I screech.

They roll in the dirt several times until Vane is on his feet again, his boot pressed against the person's neck.

The person on the ground, with the Dark One peering over him, laughs, though the sound is strangled beneath the sole of Vane's boot.

"Roc?" Vane says.

The other man grips Vane's foot and then shoves him back. Vane stumbles. Roc is up again and dusting off his trousers.

"The fuck are you doing?" Vane says, his voice devoid of any excitement to see his brother.

"Testing your reflexes." Roc runs a hand through his dark hair. "You're shit at it, apparently. You should have heard me coming."

"I was fucking busy!"

Roc turns to me and a breath gets lodged in my throat. I'm still a little warm and fuzzy from the wine, and Roc's attention on me makes me warmer.

Because holy stars, he is hot.

I barely remember him when he was here last, back when he cut off my brother's hand for some perceived slight with Wendy Darling.

I can still hear Jas's terror and later his groans of pain as Smee tended to the wound.

"Hi," Roc says, "And you are?"

"Cherry." I'm not dressed for meeting new company! Definitely not Vane's infamous older brother.

He's an inch or two taller than Vane, which would put him closer to Peter Pan's height. He's lean like Vane though, and has a certain litheness to him that would probably serve him well if he decided to become an assassin or a thief.

Or maybe he already is.

Honestly I don't really know much about Roc other than he's psychotic and known in the Isles as the Devourer of Men.

Jas is terrified of him.

I've never seen him twitch just at the mention of another man quite like he does with Roc.

Does Jas know his arch nemesis has returned to Neverland?

I might want to return to his end of the island just to be the one to tell him to see the blood drain from his face.

I am still nursing a grudge against my brother. And this might satisfy some of it.

Roc reaches over and takes my fingers in his hand, and

bends my knuckles to his mouth. He plants a lingering kiss and keeps his gaze trained on me.

I shiver.

While he and Vane share the same bone structure—sharp cheekbones, a cut jaw, and full lips—his eyes are bright green.

Heat builds in my chest. I could get used to this kind of attention.

"Christ," Vane says and bats his brother away from me. "Not that one."

"She's gorgeous though. Look at all those freckles. And you know how I feel about red heads."

"She's Hook's little sister."

"Even more of a reason."

"What the fuck are you doing here, Roc?"

"I'm sure you know."

They look at one another and I swear the air between them whirls with heat.

Why do I get the feeling that Roc's challenge is barbed? There is a double meaning behind his words.

Vane narrows his eyes.

"What did the fae queen tell you?"

"Ahhh see. You do know." Roc smooths over his hair and then hooks his arm around my shoulders. He smells like expensive cologne and sweet liquor and burning tobacco.

"Hi Cherry," he says down to me.

"Hi."

"Where would a man find Peter Pan around here?"

"Roc," Vane says in warning.

Up ahead, the Treehouse is starting to light up in the coming night. I can already hear music playing from behind the house where the Lost Boys are probably already half drunk.

"I'm sure he's somewhere in the house," I tell Roc. "Probably with Winnie."

"The new Darling."

I swallow. "Yes."

Roc looks over his shoulder at his brother and says, "How adorable. Take me to them, if you please."

12

WINNIE

I'VE BEEN FLOATING IN THE LAGOON FOR COUNTLESS MINUTES, maybe hours, with Peter Pan watching me like a guard on the shore.

As soon as I was on my feet after Smee left, he took my hand, dragged me from the house, through the forest and to the lagoon.

"Get in," he had ordered.

"I'm fine," I protested to which he said, "Get in the goddamn water Darling before I toss you in."

With a huff, I peeled off my clothes and waded in and though I don't like to admit when Peter Pan is right, as soon as the water was lapping around my shoulders, I felt infinitely better.

Now I'm on my back floating and even though I've been in the water forever, my fingers aren't even pruned.

"Why don't you come in?" I call to Pan.

"The lagoon and I have an understanding," he answers.

I roll over and tread water so I can look at him on the

shore. He's got his back propped against a large rock that sits on the edge of the woods. One of his legs is stretched out in front of him, the other bent at the knee, his arm draped over it.

His feet are bare.

There is nothing quite so intimate as the bare feet of a myth.

"What sort of understanding?"

"The one where I don't get in."

More secrets between him and the island. I know his first memories are of the lagoon and that he believes it's the lagoon that birthed him.

I know he's afraid of losing his shadow again and that probably he thinks it's the lagoon that gave it to him in the first place.

Peter Pan is ancient but even he is afraid of something, but how odd that he's afraid of a lagoon and an island laying down judgement.

Because even if he won't admit it, somehow I know that to be true.

I think Peter Pan might be unconsciously worried that while he reclaimed his shadow, he no longer deserves it.

My stomach growls again and I'm reminded we never had our pancake breakfast.

"Are you hungry, Darling?" Pan asks.

"I could eat," I say.

"Come out." He stands up and grabs my dress from the sand and gives it a shake.

"But the water is so nice," I complain.

"Darling." He tilts his head in a way that promises punishment. "Don't make me repeat myself."

I know there's nothing he can do, considering he refuses to get in and I like playing games with him. I think secretly he likes playing games too so long as he wins. But I'm ravenous in a way that I've never been before, even when I was starving back at home, so I don't think I could play very long.

"Fine," I say and sink my feet into the cool sandy bottom of the lagoon and make my way to the shore.

When I walk out, water runs down my arms, down my torso and follows the V of my thighs. My hair is heavy and wet and sticks to my breasts.

Peter Pan's eyes are drinking me in.

"We could linger for a while," I suggest. "I'm hungry for something else, too."

"You are always hungry for cock, Darling. But you will never be able to keep up with me if you don't feed yourself something other than dessert."

"When you say 'dessert', are you referring to Lost Boy cum or pancakes?"

He snorts and holds up my dress. He has it bunched in his hands so all I have to do is thread my arms in as he pushes it over my head.

I wiggle my hips so the thin cotton will sink over my hips. Pan lets out an appreciative growl.

"There will be plenty of time to fill you up with Lost Boy cum, Darling. But right now, you need meat and potatoes. Something to stick to your bones. Come."

"I'm trying." I give him a devilish grin.

"Is that the game we're playing then?"

I don't know what's gotten into me. I am 100% a sex-positive kind of girl. I like sex and I don't try to hide that. But I'm not usually so damn needy for it.

Or maybe it's Peter Pan I'm needy for.

Pan scoops me up and tosses me over his shoulder.

"Hey!"

The wolf barrels out of the woods and yips at Pan.

"I warned her," Pan tells the wolf. "She will obey me and so will you."

The wolf yips.

I'm not sure what that means but Pan seems satisfied with the response.

He starts away from the lagoon.

But he doesn't go toward the treehouse. Instead he goes toward town.

"I thought we were getting food?"

"We are," he says. "It's about time I show my face in Darlington Port. Remind them all who rules this land."

It isn't until I hear the distant hum of a small city that Pan puts me down. I straighten out my dress and realize I'm bare foot. But so is Pan. I guess there's something wild about us both.

The dirt path from the woods connects to a road that goes north and south. But across it is a cobblestone road that spills downhill into a town.

Darlington Port, I guess. I can hear the rattle of wagon wheels over the stones. People shouting and laughing. The toll of a distant bell. The clashing of metal on metal and the smell of burning iron.

It wasn't that long ago that I lived a normal life in a normal town in the normal world.

But however long I've been on Neverland and at the treehouse, it's somehow wiped away what was normal and replaced it with something new.

Because being here in Darlington, I feel like a tourist in

a novelty shop. Like I want to oohh and ahhh around every corner.

I suppose it doesn't hurt that Darlington Port is very much like a 19th century Dutch Colonial town with white stucco buildings with exposed timber beams and crooked little stoops with colorful awnings and goods displayed in shop windows.

"You've been keeping this from me this entire time?! This is wonderful!" I say up to Pan and he smiles down at me.

"I suppose it does have it's charm."

We pass a bakery and a man out front is sweeping the stone stoop, the sign in his front window reading CLOSED in big red letters.

When he sees Pan, he stops sweeping, bows his head and keeps his eyes on the stone. "Never King," he mumbles.

Pan ignores him.

Across the street is a book shop and a stationary next to it and a shoe shop next to that. Only the latter is open.

"Do you have money?" I ask Pan. "I could use shoes." I wiggle my toes on the cold cobblestone.

"Of course."

Something sweet bites at the air and on the tip of my tongue and a second later, Pan holds out his hand to reveal a pile of gold coins.

"Holy shit. How did you...where..."

I would have noticed if he was carrying a pile of heavy coins in his pants. Trust me. I notice everything that goes on in his pants.

"A perk of the shadow," he admits. "I can make anything appear."

I gaze up at him. I sense there are practically stars in my eyes. "You are amazing."

He breathes out through his nose and the corner of his mouth lifts. "Go on. Take a few and buy yourself some shoes, Darling."

He doesn't have to tell me twice. I pluck a few coins out, having no idea what the worth is or the cost of shoes, and then push through the heavy wooden door on the shoe shop. A bell dings above us and the salesman calls out a hello before he spots Peter Pan and the wolf beside us.

"Good god." The man sinks to one knee. "I had no idea you were... Apologies, Never King. What an honor to have you in my shop."

"My..." Pan looks over at me and a wrinkle appears between his brows. "Darling needs a new pair of shoes. Could you assist her?"

"Of course." The man stands upright. He eyes the wolf, opens his mouth like he means to protest the big hairy beast and then thinks better of it. "What will the lady desire?"

"Something simple will do." I look around the shop. It's small and cozy, but there are displays everywhere on the shelves that line the walls and on the little square tables that dot the room.

I make my way to the shelf on my left and the floor creaks loudly beneath me and then the wolf's claws click and scrape as he follows.

"What do you think?" I ask him as I pluck a ballet flat from the shelf and hold it out.

The wolf says, *No good for running.*

I peer down at him. "Who says I need to run?"

You should always be prepared to run.

"I agree with him," Pan says behind me.

"Fine." I return the flat to the shelf and then pick up a brown leather boot with laces. "This then?"

"Better," Pan and the wolf say at once.

"Do you have this in a seven?" I ask and the salesman nods and hurries to the back.

"Why are you both worried about me running?" I ask.

Pan is leaning against one of the floor-to-ceiling shelves on the other side of the shop, his arms crossed over his chest. He's unmoving, but there is still an aura about him that he could break bones quickly, with barely any effort.

If Peter Pan was intimidating before, now with his shadow, he's...he's...

It's impossible to find the right words to describe how it feels to be near him now.

Like trying to describe the way a hurricane feels two days before it reaches land. The air is different and you can feel the impending destruction maybe in your belly, maybe in your soul. But you can't touch it with your hands and so it doesn't feel real until the carnage is lying around your feet.

Peter Pan is like that. Like a hurricane.

The wolf comes around a display to look up at me and he snaps me out of my reverie.

Need shoes to run, he tells me.

The salesman comes barreling through a swinging door, a black box in hand. "Here we go!" He sets the box down and pulls over a chair and gestures for me to sit in it.

"Do you have socks?" I ask.

He yanks a pair off a rack, tears off the tag and hands them to me. They're made of soft creamy cotton with a little bit of a slouch to them.

With the socks on, I slip on the boots and then tighten up the laces and take a test walk across the store.

"Holy shit. These are amazing."

The salesman beams. "I only craft the best. I was an

apprentice of The Shoemaker."

"The shoemaker?" I ask.

"Renowned Shoemaker in the Seven Isles," Pan answers. "Taught by the elves."

"Right. *The elves.* Of course." I will never get used to the absurdity of this place. And I suspect I've only just scratched the surface.

I lift up my foot to inspect the boots. "Well The Shoemaker and the elves clearly know how to do what they do. I'm glad he passed on that knowledge to you too," I tell the salesman.

He nods and clasps his hands together. "I'm so glad you like them."

"How much do we owe you?" Pan asks.

"Oh no. No." The salesman shakes his head. "I couldn't take money from the Never King."

"You can and you will. How much?"

"I really mustn't—"

I go over to the older man, grab his hand. The second our skin touches, his expression goes blank and his eyes wide. "Our thanks," I tell him and drop several coins into his open palm.

He nods numbly and then immediately sinks to his knees.

"Thank you. Thank you to you both. What a blessing tonight has been."

Peter Pan pushes away from the shelf and frowns down at the man. "Why are you bowing to her?"

I laugh and push Pan toward the door. "Let the man do what he wants, Never King."

Still he scowls. "Only I will be on my knees for you." He takes my hand in his and yanks me outside into the warm darkness, the wolf following behind.

"Not just you," I remind him.

He sighs. "Yes, fine. Vane, the twins, and myself. Better?"

I frown. "I'm not sure. Why don't you show me what you mean?"

There is a deep rumble in his chest. "Darling, I will not—"

My stomach makes another loud complaint, cutting Pan off. He lets our argument drop and pulls me up the next street, then turns us down a wider thoroughfare where more nightlife abounds.

There is energy here. I've never been to New Orleans or Bourbon Street, but I imagine this is what it must feel like surrounded by buildings that feel old while the people and their music fill up the cracks and crevices with laughter and revelry.

Pan nods at a tavern halfway down the street. A sign hangs from the roof ledge that reads OX & MEAD in old English lettering.

Is that the name of the tavern or the food they offer?

I'm not eating ox. I was hoping for a burger and fries.

I need to eat too, the wolf says beside us and then takes off at a sprint.

When Pan and I enter the tavern, we're greeted by a din of conversation and the quiet song of a lute. Circular tables are spread over the room with a bar on the right and booths that line the back. Giant arched windows let in the warm light of the lampposts outside.

It takes the tavern a few seconds to notice who is standing just inside the door.

And then the entire place goes quiet and all eyes are on us.

13

PETER PAN

I FORGOT WHAT IT WAS TO COMMAND A ROOM.

I've made myself scarce since I lost my shadow.

An amateur mistake.

That changes now.

My shadow looms just below my skin and then expands outward behind me despite the direction of the light in the room.

The Neverland Life Shadow needs no light to exist and I can feel it wanting to make its presence known.

It and I have a long way to go to become one again, but it is as excited as I am to show Neverland who holds the power once again.

And the shadow blooms outward, engulfing the room.

The golden glow of the lanterns burns brighter while the shadows grow darker.

Suddenly chairs are scraping loudly over the hardwood floor as people quickly climb to their feet and then sink to their knees.

That's more like it.

I had intended to come here to put food in Darling's belly, but now I realize there is more work to be done.

"The shadow has returned to its rightful place." I walk among their bent bodies. "I am the Never King and the heart of Neverland. Never doubt that."

They keep their heads bowed but a murmur goes through the crowd and then a man in the back pipes up. "We never doubted you, my king."

I can tell he's lying. They all doubted me. Hell, even I doubted me.

I am still full of doubt.

Without thinking it, I reach for Darling's hand. As soon as hers is in mine, she gives me a squeeze.

I needed her reassurance.

I needed her reassurance?

I turn back to the tavern.

"Now let us celebrate," I tell them. "Return to your dinners and your revelries and let your king dine among you."

They lurch upright. There is a shuffle of chairs and fabric, a clatter of dishes as they return to their tables. And I pull Darling to the back of the room to a booth hidden partially in shadow.

I can't shake the feeling that I want to retreat again.

I don't like this one fucking bit.

I need a fucking drink.

A server comes over dressed in the Ox & Mead green livery. Her hair is plaited down the center of her head and several errant curls have escaped to frame her face.

"Welcome to the Ox & Mead, my king. So good to have you." She smiles and gives me a clumsy bow. "What can I get for you?"

"I need liquor. Dark. Any will do."

"We have an excellent whisky from Winterland that I think you'll appreciate." She turns to Darling. "And for the Darling?"

Of course she and everyone here knows about Darling. Gossip in Darlington Port may not be as prevalent as it is in the fae court, but they still talk.

"Burger and French fries?" Darling asks.

The excited uptick in her voice is unmistakable.

"Ummm..." The server holds a pencil over a notepad, unsure of what to write. "French...*fries*?"

"Matchsticks," I tell the girl.

"Right. Of course." She scribbles that down.

"And a meat sandwich." I turn to Darling. "What do you like on your burgers?"

"Lettuce?"

I can't help but laugh. "We don't put leaves on food here."

She grumbles. "Pickles?"

"That we do have."

"Ketchup?"

"Tomato syrup," I translate to the server.

She nods and continues scribbling.

"Tomato syrup?" Darling screws up her mouth, aghast. "What in the hell is that?"

"It's sweet like your ketchup. Just trust me."

"Fine." She looks up at the server. "A meat sandwich please with pickles and tomato syrup."

"Coming right up!" The girl practically jogs away and disappears to the kitchen.

"I'm a little terrified of what will come out of that kitchen." Darling gets in close to my side and I immediately like her nearness.

"Your realm feeds you in fake food and processed garbage and you're afraid of Neverland tomato sauce?"

"You said syrup."

I like her wonder and her doubtfulness. She is adorable when she's unsure because most of the time she likes to pretend she has everything in hand.

My drink arrives by the barkeep and he says nothing as he sets it down and spins and hurries away.

I sniff the glass for poisons. Neverland is full of my enemies now. I can never be too sure.

There is only the spiciness of Winterland and the sharpness of the alcohol.

I take a sip. The heat is welcomed as it pools in my gut.

"Let me try." Darling takes a drink. "Ohhh." Her mouth pops open while her eyes squint shut. "That's like drinking Christmas in a glass. But heavy on the nog. Did she say it's from Winterland?"

"Yes."

"And what is that?"

"Another island."

"There are seven, right?"

"There are." I take another drink. There is likely no way I will ever be drunk again. The shadow won't allow it and I suppose it's just as well, but I will enjoy the burn just the same.

"What are the others besides Neverland and Winterland?" Darling asks.

"Winterland and Summerland are on opposite ends of the island chain. Between them is Darkland, Vane's homeland. Neverland. Pleasureland—"

Darling chokes on her second drink of my glass.

"Lostland and Everland."

"Did you say Pleasureland?"

"I did."

"But...how?"

"It is a place where all your pleasure fantasies come true."

"I need to go there."

"You absolutely do not."

She frowns up at me and pushes out her puffy bottom lip. "Why not?"

"Because it is a wild and reckless place and addictive like a drug. You go to Pleasureland, you don't come back from it."

Darling lets that sink in.

"I still can't believe any of this is real. When my mom told me about you and the Lost Boys growing up, I thought it was a story she read in a book. Now I'm in an alternate realm fucking a myth about to be served tomato syrup."

My hand immediately goes to her thigh and I push up her dress to feel the warm flesh between her legs. "Fucking a myth? I think the myth is fucking you."

She snorts. "Keep telling yourself that."

I smile at her. She is a fucking delight.

Her food comes out fresh and steaming. The French fries, as she calls them, are golden brown and glisten from the oil and salt. The sandwich—*burger*—sits between two slices of homemade bread and the rich tomato sauce drips from it.

"Oh god. This looks amazing." Darling pulls the plate closer and tests a matchstick that she runs through the pool of sauce on the side. The fried potato crunches between her teeth and I know the instant the tomato syrup hits her taste buds because her eyes pop open.

"See?" I can't help myself.

"Wow." She swallows and grabs another and looks at

the server still standing there waiting for a dismissal. "Really, wow. Thank you..."

"Darlina."

Darling stops chewing.

"Sorry," the server says. "Maybe that's weird? It's a popular name on Neverland."

If it was, I didn't know. Then again, I'm so far removed from what life is on my island.

"Nice to meet you, Darlina," Darling says. "And thank you for this delicious meal."

The server dips down like she means to curtsy and then thinks better of it. "My pleasure," she says and then darts away.

"Darlina?" Darling whispers to me. "They've adopted a name like my surname?"

"The Darling stories go back generations," I tell her. "I'm not surprised."

"But I thought we were your villain or whatever?"

"No, Darling." I steal one of her fries. "I am the villain here."

14

ROC

Peter Pan and his Darling are nowhere to be found and my patience is growing thin.

Behind the house, a party is well underway. Plenty of Lost Boys and girls drinking and carousing. I would join them if it hadn't been years and years since I saw my baby brother.

He pours us each a drink at the bar in the loft. He doesn't ask what I want, but I'm sure he remembers I prefer bourbon.

Time may have stretched between us, but there are some things brothers never forget.

He brings the glass over to me and sits in the leather chair across from the couch where I'm lounging in the crook.

The loft is quiet. The twins disappeared with Cherry as soon as I arrived.

I suppose my reputation precedes me. The twins were not with Pan last I was here. They came much later.

"I like what you've done with the place," I tell Vane.

He takes a healthy drink of his liquor and barely winces as it burns down his throat.

"Whatever your plan is," Vane says, "I won't let you see it through."

I smile at him and try not to let the irritation reach my eyes. My baby brother has changed and I'm not entirely sure by how much.

A pinch? A mile? A fucking cavern's length?

"Let me ask you a question." I sit forward and prop my elbows on my knees. "If it came down to choosing between Peter Pan and me, who would you choose?"

"If it came down to it, why would you make me?"

Something sinister glitters in his black eye. I vividly recall him flailing beneath me as I tried to tend to the wound. I remember the paleness of his skin, the hollowness of his cheeks, and the very real fear that he wouldn't survive.

He and I are not like most men. But even special men are sometimes no match for a shadow.

"Did you know?" I ask him.

The quiet grows loud.

"Did you, Vane?"

"I only just found out." He drains the rest of the glass and sets it down hard on the table between us. "And don't pretend you were slighted. You barely knew Wendy."

"I knew her enough." I upend my own glass and welcome the alcohol's sweetness and its heat. I need more. I need so much more. "The fae queen shared a memory she plucked from a Darling's head." I reach into my pocket and pull out a handful of peanuts. "As you know, memories are passed down by blood."

"Yes, I know."

"And Peter Pan left Wendy as she begged for his help and then begged him to seek mine."

"You had already left, remember? After she jilted you."

"Because of fucking James Hook."

"You and your mountain of enemies."

"Don't make me add you to the pile."

He lurches upright. "Why do you fucking care? That was ages ago. Don't pretend like he took the great love of your life."

"Would you have left Lainey?"

The look on my baby brother's face is the same look a man might have right after he's been slapped across the face with a sledgehammer.

I almost regret it.

Almost.

"Do not bring her into this." His violet eye goes black. "Wendy is not Lainey."

I am not my brother. I don't feel emotion like he does. But I can almost imagine it when we talk of our little sister.

I didn't want to dig up old graves, but I've already dug too far.

"Peter Pan does what he wants. Should there be no consequences for him?"

Vane grits his teeth. "And what do you call what you do?"

"I have rules, baby brother. Peter Pan has none."

"Rules." He scoffs and turns away. "Rules only you know. Rules that you seem to pull out of thin air."

I follow him down the main staircase.

"When have I ever left an innocent girl to fend for herself?"

"Dytus," he says.

Christ.

Dytus was a girl from the Umbrage that used to follow us around like a lost little puppy.

"That was a unique situation," I say. "I ran out of time."

"And yet the result was the same."

The Lost Boys send up a cheer in the backyard. When we reach the foyer, the hot orange glow of the bonfire spills across the floor through the open back doors. There is the distinct smell of campfire and burning tobacco in the air.

Vane goes to the large front door and pulls it open and holds it. "Go, before he comes back."

"If you won't choose," I tell him, "I'll make you choose."

"I clearly already have, Roc."

"You wound me, brother."

He just stares at me with his black eyes.

I want to slap him across the face and wake him up. Either that or kidnap him and cart him off this godforsaken island.

I don't want to fight him but I will if I have to.

"Change your mind," I tell him.

All of the levity is gone from my voice and I let him see it.

He is steeled and the wood of the door creaks in his hand as his grip tightens on a freshly glued repair.

"All right." I smile at him. "In that case," I crack one of the peanuts and let the shell rain down around my boots, "you should know, I traveled with the Remaldi family."

My baby brother's entire demeanor shifts. His mouth parts open, betraying a sliver of surprise.

I bite into a peanut and look out into the night. "They've waited long enough for the return of their shadow." Another peanut cracks in my hand. "It's rightfully theirs."

"Shadows belong to no man. Only the land."

"I think Peter Pan would disagree with you."

His nostrils flare. He knows I'm right.

"I suppose I'll head into town and see what kind of trouble I can get into. In the meantime, please do reconsider your position. I'll give you until sunrise to bring the shadow to us. If you don't—"

"You'll what, Roc?"

I pop another peanut in my mouth and dust the shells from my hands. "I'll let the time run out."

15

PETER PAN

Darling devours her meal in record time. I don't think she comes up for a full breath before she's licking her fingers clean of the tomato sauce, one fingertip at a time.

I can't help but imagine it's something else she's cleaning off and I'm instantly hard.

"What is your verdict?" I ask her trying to distract myself and my rogue cock.

"It was better than I expected." She takes a long drink of the Winterland whisky and winces as it goes down. "I'm feeling tons better."

"Yes, let's talk about your care and—"

The tavern door creaks open and because I like to know everything about my surroundings, I am drawn to the newcomers.

And the moment I see that bright blond hair, my insides chill.

Remaldi royalty and several of their guards.

It doesn't take much to connect the dots.

Tilly summoned the Crocodile. The Crocodile is from Darkland.

The Darkland royals probably saw an opening to retrieve their dark shadow.

Vane will give the shadow back, I'm sure of it. But now is not the fucking time.

There are two guards who keep two paces back and three of the royal family with the queen at the head. I don't recognize the other two women, but they're younger than she is, which means they are much, much younger than me.

Giselle spots me in an instant. I am hard to miss.

"Christ," I mutter when she starts over.

"What is it?" Darling asks. She follows my line of sight and goes rigid beside me when she lands her gaze on Giselle.

The air shifts. Did the wolf return from his hunt already?

I don't see him.

I look over at Darling as the energy in the air mounts.

The fuck is that?

I can *feel* her.

I can feel...

Oh fuck.

"Peter Pan!" Giselle says.

The Darkland queen stops at the head of our table and clasps her hands in front of her. Though Neverland has always been more tropical than arctic, Giselle is wearing a fur shawl made of what looks like a wolf's pelt.

Beneath that, a black dress skims her body in skeins of silk.

Her blond hair is woven into several thick plaits that are pinned around her head like a crown.

She knows better than to wear an actual crown on Neverland.

Behind her is a young woman who might be twenty-two or fifty, depending on how she ages. She's swearing the Remaldi royal crest and she has the Remaldi blond hair, so I assume she's a princess.

Beside her is another girl, younger still.

"The fuck do you want?" I say to Giselle.

I need to get her out of here.

I need Vane and the twins.

"Can a queen not visit another island? See the sights? Maybe sample the island's finest goods?"

She rocks her shoulders back purposefully pushing out her chest. The shawl is clasped at the base of her throat, but her dress is cut low exposing the swell of her breasts. The silk of her dress is thin and her nipples are pebbled against the material.

"I can assure you," I say. "There's plenty of other fine goods on *other* islands. So you can kindly fuck off mine."

Her ruby red lips screw up in a lecherous grin. "But Peter—"

"You heard him," Darling says.

When I look over at Darling again, her head is bowed and her hair is hanging in her face.

That energy is crawling up my spine.

"And who is this whore?" Giselle asks. "Peter Pan, you never were discerning enough." She comes closer to my side of the booth and leans into me, putting her arm around my shoulders, her mouth at my ear so she can whisper, "Perhaps we go back to my ship and—"

Darling leaps over the table, a knife in her hand and rams it into Giselle's throat.

Blood paints the air.

The tavern is immediately in chaos.

Giselle stumbles back, groping at her throat as blood mats the fur of her shawl.

The princess goes pale, but she's quick on her feet and pulls a sword from the sheath at her hips.

But Darling has her by the wrist in a second and blackness eats away at the princess's skin and pulses through her veins.

She chokes on the darkness. Blood vessels burst around her eyes.

The Remaldi guards come at Darling next, but I'm already on my feet.

I yank the blade from Giselle's neck and ram it into the eye socket of the first guard, then boot the second one in the chest. He slams into a table behind him and drinks spill to the floor, glasses shattering into a million pieces.

"Darling!" I shout.

She turns and looks at me.

And both of her eyes are darkest black.

"Drop her."

There is the familiar sound of a pistol arm cocked back.

I know that voice.

I know it very well.

After all, it sounds not unlike Vane's voice.

They are brothers, after all.

I turn to find the Crocodile in the middle of the tavern, a liberated pistol in his hand. He has the barrel pointed at Darling.

"Drop her," he repeats calmly.

The Remaldi princess is still choking for air, but the blackness is starting to envelop her face.

She doesn't have much time left.

"Roc." I hold out my hands to show him I'm unarmed. "Put the fucking gun down."

He pulls a pocket watch out of his pocket, pops open the front. "She has five seconds. Starting now."

Five seconds isn't enough time.

I can't kill Roc.

Vane would kill me.

But I can do a great many things without tearing out a man's heart.

I dart across the room in flight and barrel into Roc. We crash into the bar, then topple over it and slam to the floor on the other side.

I'm up in a second and he swings with a bottle of scotch. I duck. He misses. I catch the bottle when he comes back around and reach for the well of my power.

It's been so long but the second I tap into it, it races through my veins and adrenaline beats at my ribs.

The bottle lets out a loud POP and then it bursts into firecracker flowers.

Roc looks down at the petals now crushed in his hand and his teeth grit together, his eyes flashing bright.

I can't help but smile.

And Roc uses my prideful distraction to punch me in the fucking face.

When the ringing fades from my ears, he's already leaping over the bar.

I fly out after him.

The last of the tavern-goers scream and scatter for the door.

Roc grabs a chair by the back, lifts it over his head, and whacks Darling with the base.

"No!" I shout.

Darling and the Remaldi princess slam to the floor.

I snatch a steak knife from a table and send it sailing across the room, aimed right for Roc's head.

But he catches it at the last second. Plucks it from the air, just like that.

Then he reaches for Darling and takes a fistful of her hair and yanks her to her feet.

He puts her back to his chest and wraps his arm around her, the sharp edge of the blade pressed against her throat.

"Don't do this," I tell him.

He nods at the princess splayed on the floor. "Fix her."

"It doesn't work like that."

He presses the blade against Darling's throat and blood beads beneath it.

Through gritted teeth, I tell him, "I'm going to kill you."

"Fix the princess. It's in your best interest and mine if you fix her."

I don't doubt him. Roc isn't stupid. And he plays by strategy, not emotion.

There is a dead queen lying on the tavern floor and a princess not far behind. I'm not sure about the youngest girl, but I think it's safe to assume she's dead too.

"Fine," I tell Roc. "Let me go to her."

Darling's black eyes are trained on me.

I have no time to question how she got Neverland's Death Shadow or how much it's taken over. No time to contemplate the consequences of her having it.

But when the corner of her mouth lifts in a mischievous little smirk, I know I'm in fucking trouble.

Because there will be consequences.

There've already begun.

She wraps her hand around Roc's forearm, her other around his opposite wrist.

On any other day, under any other circumstance, he would be stronger than her.

But it's not any other day.

Blackness creeps out of her grip, up his arm. He hisses in pain and instinctively steps back. She shoves out, shifting the blade from her flesh, then immediately ducks and spins and jabs him with his own hand.

His eyes go wide as blood spills from his mouth and pours down his neck soaking into his shirt.

"Darling," I call.

Roc staggers back and slumps against the wall.

"Darling. We have to go. Right fucking now."

Roc chokes and the sound is wet and garbled.

"Darling!"

She finally looks at me and it's like I'm in a fever dream.

I am looking at her, but I can feel her seeing me too, and for the first time in my entire immortal life, I sense the shadows connecting, like two mirrors pointed at each other.

"Come," I tell her.

And though her eyes are still black and she's covered in blood, she smiles up at me, takes my offered hand and follows me out the door.

16

PETER PAN

As soon as we're under the Neverland sky and breathing in the fresh night air, I scoop Darling into my arms and take flight. She hooks her hands behind my neck and rests her head against my shoulder. She says nothing all the way back to the treehouse.

I can hear the party underway when I land, but I can't tell where Vane and the twins are just yet.

I need to get Darling somewhere safe so I can figure out what to do next.

I push quietly through the front door and find the foyer empty. The sconces that follow the curving staircase up to the loft are lit and flickering light casts odd shadows around the space.

The twins are in the kitchen. Bash is trying to cheer Cherry up with a sweet tart. Kas is laughing at something his brother said.

Of course The Dark One is silent. I'm anticipating him

appearing practically out of thin air to analyze me and Darling covered in blood.

Not yet.

I can't face him yet.

I fly up to the loft and then down the hall, more grateful than ever that I have the ability back.

But at the last second, I realize I made a grave error.

Vane is in the library.

"There you are," he says as I land outside my tomb door. His boots are heavy on the hardwood floor and an uneven board pops beneath his weight as he comes out to greet me. "Where did you go?" he asks.

"Town," I tell him and pull open the door to the turret, keeping my back to him so he doesn't see Darling.

When he finds out she killed his brother...

The thing they don't tell you about love is that sometimes you are forced to pick between two impossible versions.

Vane or Darling? I could never choose.

I don't want to.

"Is that blood?" Vane asks.

"I got into a fight with a drunk in a tavern. It's not mine."

"And Winnie?" His voice drops a decibel and I pause at the top of the winding staircase, my gut lurching at the emotion threaded through his voice.

There is too much caring these days.

And I don't know how to handle it.

I thought getting my shadow back would solve all of my problems, but I forgot just how many problems I have. And that not all of them can be solved with *power*.

"Sleeping," I tell him over my shoulder even though her

eyes are wide open. "I'm laying her down in my room. Don't disturb us."

"Pan," he starts, but I kick the door shut with my boot and seal him out.

On the top stair, I hold my breath, anticipating him ignoring my command.

But he doesn't come and I'm not sure if I should be relieved or ashamed that I'm keeping this secret from him.

He will never forgive us.

Even if it's been years since he spoke to his brother, even if he holds a great deal of loyalty to me, I am not his blood.

My footsteps echo back to us as I carry Darling down the stairs and then into my tomb. I don't even have to think about the light before it's flicking on of its own accord and washing away the shadows.

My power is growing and settling into place.

But I can't fucking enjoy it.

Not yet anyway.

As soon as I lay Darling in my bed, she curls into her side and tucks her hands into her chest.

"I feel funny," she says.

No shit.

Her eyes are still black.

Where the fuck did she get the shadow?

And better yet, how the fuck is she holding on to it?

Now her fainting earlier is making much more sense. I'm surprised she's not writhing in pain. And yet, everything about Darling, from the moment I first met her, has proven to be different than what I expected.

I have to fix her.

I have to fix this.

"I think I'll take a nap," she says.

"I'll watch over you," I tell her.

She smiles at me and closes her eyes.

Within moments, her breathing is evened out and I finally exhale with relief and then drop into the wingback.

I don't break my promises to Darling, so I watch over her while she rests.

There is nothing sinister or terrifying about her right now other than the blood still peppered on her skin.

If I can look beyond that, she looks like an innocent girl with pale cheeks and bony shoulders and a mess of thick, dark hair.

I go to her and sit on the edge of the bed and tuck a lock of hair behind her ear.

She turns into my hand and breathes in deeply.

My shadow takes notice and writhes beneath the surface.

How the hell did I miss this?

The fucking wolf muddled my senses. I thought I was feeling his energy, but now I think it was the shadow lurking beneath Darling's eyes.

She won't last like this. The shadow will burn through her soon enough.

Vane can barely control his shadow and he isn't even human.

"What am I to do with you, Darling?" I whisper.

I stand and pace the room, hands clasped behind my head as I think. We can remove the shadow if I can find a temporary vessel. It won't be easy, but it can be done. And Vane—perhaps I can convince him it wasn't her fault.

Then again, I had plenty of opportunity to save Roc and I didn't. I was too worried about Darling.

When I come back around to pace the length of the room, I find Darling floating up to the ceiling.

"Darling!" I shout and then realize I'm a fucking idiot.

She lurches awake, realizes she's practically on the ceiling, and screeches.

I'm beneath her in an instant when she drops. She lands with an *umph* in my arms.

"What...how..." She looks up at me with wide eyes.

"It's all right," I tell her, but it isn't, and she knows it.

"What just happened? How did I get down here?" She grips me tightly by the biceps. "Why do I keep losing track of time, Pan?"

Panic turns her voice raspy.

I have never wanted to shoulder the burden of someone else's fear as badly as this.

"It's all right," I tell her again.

"What happened?"

"Darling—"

"Tell me, Pan."

I set her to her feet. "It would seem you've somehow claimed the Neverland Death Shadow."

"What?!" she yells.

17

HOOK

My arm is throbbing.

My throat is dry.

I can't fucking sleep.

Back and forth across my office. Again and again and again.

The Crocodile is on Neverland soil.

Every possession within my office has been lined up precisely, every shelf dusted and gleaming. There is nothing else to distract me.

I'm going to kill him.

Just as soon as I figure out how.

"Jas," Smee says. "Why don't you try lying down?"

"Lie down?" I turn to face her. "Lie down, Smee?!"

She sighs and pushes a boot off the wall to propel herself forward. She plucks a decanter from the bottle collection on the cart and then fills a glass with scotch.

"Drink," she orders.

"How are you so fucking calm?"

Nothing rattles Smee.

I envy her unflappable disposition. I particularly envy her unflappable disposition when I feel so fucking *flapped*.

"Worrying will get you nowhere," she tells me.

"I'm not worried!"

She cants her head and a thick loc slides over her shoulder. "What would you call it?"

I upend the glass. I'm already three in. I can't be drunk when the Crocodile is on the island. But three glasses have barely touched the knot between my shoulder blades or the constant churning in my gut.

I'm going to kill him.

Strategize a plan and then find him and then kill him.

"Jas," Smee says again.

"What?"

"He's not here for you."

"But he'll make a pit stop, I'm sure of it." I start pacing again. "Just to terrorize me. Remind me I touched what was his. As if he owned her."

Smee returns to the open balcony door and leans against the frame, hands in her pockets.

"You *did* kidnap Wendy Darling," she reminds me.

"Smee!"

She lifts a shoulder.

I grumble and turn away. "You're not here to point out my dubious past."

"Am I not?" She laughs. "I must have misunderstood my job duties."

I reach the far end of the room and stop.

Hearing Wendy's name conjures an image of her in my head.

When I look back on the memories, I am never quite

sure if I remember them right, because sometimes I get the distinct feeling Wendy Darling played me.

Maybe she played the Crocodile too.

Maybe pitting us all against one another was always her plan.

I'll never know.

Because Peter Pan took her back to her world and though I have no idea how many years have passed in the mortal realm, I'm quite sure it's too many to live by.

She's dead now.

The memories need to die with her.

A flare of pain races from the end of my arm clear up to my bicep.

If I didn't know any better, I'd say there was a storm coming.

"How do we kill him, Smee?" I ask over my shoulder. She's the magical expert, the traveler of the Isles.

"The hard part will be getting close enough to him and—"

Something pounds on the front door.

Smee and I look at one another. "You expecting anyone?" I ask her and she shakes her head.

I leave my office and follow the hall to the foyer. I have the pirates scouting the hills and several more near the bay. You can never be sure which way a Crocodile might come.

The pounding gets more desperate.

"I'm coming!"

I pull the door open and a body spills inside and slumps to the floor with a loud thud.

Blood splatters over my freshly polished boots and then pools on the hardwood.

"For Christ's sake!"

The man rolls to his back and my indignation dries up.

If it's possible for all of the blood to leave a man without a single cut, I suspect it's happened just now.

I can't feel my legs.

There is a needling across my shoulder blades, like a thousand pinpricks all at once.

I pull my pistol with a shaky hand.

The Crocodile looks up at me from the floor of my fucking foyer.

"Captain," he says with a devilish smirk, despite the fact he looks to be on Death's door. There's shredded white fabric wrapped several times around his throat, but it's mostly soaked in blood. More blood has covered the front of him and has run down his arms, coating his fingertips.

"The fuck are you doing here?"

He laughs but it dissolves into a cough and he struggles to his knees, sucking in air.

I cast a glance at Smee. Both her pistols are trained on him. She's never been trigger happy, but I know she won't hesitate to pull.

"Funny you should ask," the Crocodile says and then collapses to the floor again as his eyes roll back in his head.

I kick him. He snaps to.

"What. Are. You. Doing. Here?"

"Would you believe me...if...I said...I missed you?"

I stomp him in the fucking dick.

All of the air rushes out of him and he rolls into a fetal position and laughs and chokes and coughs and laughs.

"Alright," he wheezes out after several long minutes. "Nowhere...else...*to go*."

"Surely you have a ship—"

"Peter Pan and his Darling...just killed half the Remaldi royal family." He rolls to his back again and blinks up at the wrought iron chandelier. "Tried to kill me. But Holt is going to think I set him up." Another coughing fit takes over and he loses consciousness.

"What do you think?" I ask Smee.

She uncocks the hammers on her twin pistols and returns them to her holster. "Shoot him."

I retrain the pistol on his head. He's so close.

I've dreamed about this moment for ages.

He is a spider I lost sight of, a beast who slipped through the cracks.

I've been waiting for the moment he popped back up so I could squash him beneath the heel of my boot.

He's practically dead already.

But if I put a bullet between his eyes right now, he will never know who bested him.

Killing a man when he's already down? Poor form indeed.

"Jas?" Smee says.

I can barely hear her over the loud thumping of my heart.

My hand is shaking and my residual limb is a phantom ache at my side. I bring the hook up and watch it gleam in the light.

The anger returns.

Anger at what he did and what he had no right to take.

I can't kill him.

I can't let him get away with it so easily.

"Get him up." I return the pistol to my hip.

Smee gives me a look.

"We might need him," I tell her.

"Doubtful."

"I know what I'm doing! I'm no amateur, Smee."

"Then stop acting like one," she says.

"Fine. I'll get him up." I go around to his head and look down at him.

Some odd feeling comes across my chest. It's the same feeling I get when I spot land from the bow of my ship.

Excitement.

Excitement to murder him, no doubt.

I hook him beneath the arms and drag him back leaving a trail of blood.

Smee follows and watches me struggle with his weight. He's all solid muscle, corded with it from shoulder to bicep to forearms. Thick veins run over his tattooed hands.

I imagine what he must look like shirtless and immediately regret the thought.

Shirtless with my blade protruding from his ribs.

That's more like it.

I drag him to one of the spare rooms at the end of the hall and kick the door in. There's a single bed shoved into the corner, a desk and a dresser. When I built this house, I included several spare rooms despite having no plans for guests.

The room smells stale and dust swirls in the faint ray of moonlight.

Smee lets me struggle with him a little more before she finally grabs him by the legs and helps me hoist him into the bed. The mattress dips, the springs creak.

The Crocodile is in my home, in my bed.

I swallow bile and my eye starts twitching.

"Now what?" Smee asks.

"I don't know," I admit.

"We really tending to him?"

Why did he come here?

Why to me of all people? Is this another game? Arrive

on my doorstep pretending to be injured so he can slither into the shadows and ambush me when I least expect it?

The Crocodile may be ruthless, but he has no qualms about being brutal in the daylight.

No, I think if he wanted to kill me, he would do it out in the open.

"Find out how badly he's injured," I tell Smee.

"And if it's fixable?"

I lick my lips, my mouth dry. "We should keep him alive."

She wraps a hand around her hip and tilts her head, watching me with that deep wariness that only Smee can get away with. "I don't like this, Jas."

I stagger back into the wall and slouch against it, sighing loudly. "To be frank, Smee, I don't either."

She nods at me and then gets to work.

18

WINNIE

"I do not have the Death Shadow."

I'm sitting on Pan's bed, leaning against the headboard, my knees drawn to my chest. I feel like a little girl again, terrified about having the flu. I always hated throwing up and my stomach had been in knots, my body burning up and trembling. I knew it was inevitable, but still I denied it was happening.

Until it did.

"Darling," Pan says.

"There must be a mistake."

"There isn't. I watched it come out and I watched it take over."

"And? What did it do?"

His brows draw together in a concerned frown.

I'm covered in blood, so I guess it was bad. But the look he's giving me has me wondering if there is something worse than bad.

"What happened?" I ask.

He lets out a breath and then tells me everything.

I yank his door open and race up the stairs.

"Darling," he calls.

"No. I did not do that."

"Darling, wait." There is a ring of command in his words, but I ignore him and take the stairs up two at a time. I don't know what I intend to do once I'm at ground level, but I'll figure it out.

"I'm going to go to town and prove to you that it's not true," I tell him.

"You will do no such thing."

"Maybe it was an illusion. Maybe the twins were fucking with you."

"Darling."

I step out of the tomb and follow the hall to the loft. Vane is there with the twins. The twins are playing a card game and drinking. Vane is reading in one of the leather chairs.

They all look up when we enter and Vane's eyes narrow when he takes in the sight of me.

"Why is she covered in blood?"

I'm about to tell him the ridiculous theory Pan has when something shifts at the center of me.

It's something I've felt several times since I woke up in my bed earlier.

A dark thing unfurls inside of me and just like with the wolf, I swear I can hear or sense its intent.

I am here, it says.

The pressure dips in the loft. I'm cold and hot at the same time, ears ringing.

There is no way in hell I somehow, mysteriously, *magically* took on the Neverland Death Shadow.

There really must be some kind of explanation.

Vane stalks up to me and towers over me, purposefully using his size to dominate me.

That dark thing takes notice and excitement pools in my gut.

"Start fucking talking, Darling."

"Vane," Pan says in warning. "You really don't—"

I smack Vane across the face.

The sound is loud in the stillness of the loft.

And there is a deep, sick satisfaction in my gut seeing the red welt appear on his pale cheek.

What the hell is wrong with me? I'm in so much trouble.

"I'm sorry...I didn't mean—"

He grabs me around the throat and runs me back against the bar.

"Vane, for Christ's sake!" Pan says and comes up behind him.

Vane's eyes are black and the first gleam of white hair appears at his crown. "You want to play games, little Darling girl?"

I'm about to apologize—*again*—but the words are caged in my mouth and I know immediately that *thing* stops me.

The air vibrates between us, and Vane tilts his head, black eyes flashing.

Excitement blooms at the base of my throat where I can feel my heart beat thumping wildly.

All of my unease, all of my doubt and fear melts away.

And all that remains is hunger.

Not for food.

Not this time.

When I answer him, the voice that comes out of my throat is not entirely my own. "Yes, Dark One. Play me so hard it hurts."

My pussy clenches when he growls in the base of his throat and his cock digs into my thigh as he shoves me down. I reach between us and grope him through his pants. His eyes slip closed and his chest rumbles with a groan.

"Stop fucking around, Darling," he says.

"Try to make me."

His eyes pop open and then his mouth is crashing against mine. He is punishing with his lips, bruising with his mouth. His large hand grabs me roughly by the jaw, commanding the kiss as his tongue invades me, claiming me.

His cock is so hard, the thick ridge of it against my thigh practically hurts.

The kiss deepens and Vane lets his hand wander to my breast and roll my nipple between his fingers. He swallows the little cry that comes out of me at the shock of pain and then he shoves my dress up around my waist and unzips himself. His pants are barely down before he's lining himself up at my center and guiding my legs around his hips.

"Why do you do this to me, Win?" he says with a grumble, pushing in an inch just enough to tease me.

"I like it when you lose your fucking mind for me."

"You like torturing me."

He nips at my neck and I gasp at the sensation.

"Maybe I do."

He presses in another inch and I think he might be trying to prove to me that he's the one in charge of this torture.

I lock my ankles around him and put pressure on his backside trying to sink him further inside of me.

But he is an unmovable force.

Lips at my throat, he kisses gently sending goosebumps down my arms. Then he's biting again, pinching skin between his sharp incisors.

I shudder and he angles me up to him.

"Beg me, Win."

I'm dripping wet and writhing against him, the pressure building.

I just want him inside of me and a desperate little whine spills out of my throat.

"Now who's losing their mind?" he says.

"Shut up and fuck me."

"Be a good girl and beg me."

"Please," I whine, giving in. "Please fuck me, Vane."

He presses me into the bar and thrusts in deep.

"Oh fuck yeah," I say around a moan.

His hands on my ass now, he pumps in hard, banding me against the bar.

Our fucking is loud and wet and frenzied.

Sweat coats my forehead and my hair sticks to me and when I open my eyes and look over Vane's shoulder, I see them all watching. Pan and Bash and Kas. Pan is smoking a cigarette, leaning against the wall. Bash is groping himself and Kas isn't far behind.

I want them all.

All mine.

All of them to worship me and play *my* game.

"Fuck, Win," Vane says at my ear, his voice barely human.

"You gonna fill me up, Dark One?"

My nails drag down the back of his neck and he hisses into my ear. "Keep fucking doing that and you'll regret it."

I dig in deeper and feel the wetness of his blood filling the half-moon wounds left by my nails.

He abruptly pulls out of me, staggers back and leaves me panting, my dress askew.

"What the fuck?" I say.

"I warned you."

"I thought you were kidding."

Cock still out and glistening with my juices, he pulls out a cigarette and lights it. He takes a long hit.

That dark thing grows agitated.

After he blows out a breath of smoke, he says, "Start running."

"Vane," Pan warns again.

"Start running, Winnie Darling."

I right my dress. "And if I don't?"

He doesn't answer me. I suppose there is no *if*. When Vane gives a command, you best start running.

The dark thing likes the sound of that.

Likes the game.

And I like the way Vane is looking at me like he's not sure if he should be punishing me or thanking me.

I turn for the balcony and start running.

19

BASH

"NOW WHY DID YOU GO AND DO THAT?" I ASK. "I WAS ENJOYING that."

Vane takes another hit from his cigarette, his finger curled around the end at his mouth. The ember sends a shot of bright orange light over his face and his black eyes.

"Vane," Pan says again, "we need to talk."

"Not now," Vane says. "Now we teach our Darling a lesson."

"Which is what?" Pan asks.

"Yes, please enlighten us, Dark One. You tell her to run, you chase her. And what? We get left high and dry?"

"I have to agree with my brother," Kas says beside me. "Chasing is your game."

"It doesn't have to be," Vane says. He stabs the cigarette into an ashtray. "Whoever finds her first gets to pick a hole."

"Well shit. You don't have to tell me twice." I'm already

up and heading for the door. I'm not as fast as Vane is, but I've got tracking skills he doesn't.

Pan grumbles. Something has been agitating him since he came up from his tomb, but whatever it is, probably it can wait. I mean, if there's a Darling pussy to fuck, I'm fucking it.

Kas and I hit the cool outdoors together. "Bet I can find her first," he says.

"Fuck you. I'm finding her first."

He laughs as he hurries down the steps.

Above us, Pan and Vane fly through the air.

"That's cheating!" I yell to them.

"It's harder to spot tracks from the air," Kas reminds me.

"True. Which way you think she went?" We're at the edge of the yard now. We know our Darling girl. She probably went toward the lagoon. It's her favorite spot on the island.

But...she's not stupid. She probably knows we'd think to go there first.

I turn and look toward the opposite end of the island where the moonlight glows against the water of Silver Cove.

If she is a clever Darling girl...

"I say we go south."

"Worth the gamble," Kas says.

I whack him on the chest and he grunts.

"Last one there is a loser!" I yell.

Thirty yards from the treehouse, I know we made the right choice. There's a fresh break in an oak branch that hangs over the foot path leading from the house to the cove. And it's just about at the height of a Darling girl.

I put my finger over my mouth to silence my twin. He gives me a nod.

We haven't hunted like this in ages. Before we were kicked out of the palace and the court, we'd hunt the north-west side of the fae territory several times a week. Mostly it was deer to fill the smokers, sometimes grouse or duck.

It doesn't take my body or my mind much effort to go into hunter mode.

We hear a crack to our right and Kas and I share a look.

We got her now, he says.

Fucking right we do.

I hold up my fingers and count down.

Three.

Two.

One.

We dart forward, separating to funnel her in.

Another crack.

The loud sound of her breathing.

I snatch her first, catching her by the arm and whirling her around. She lets out an umph when I bring her against my chest.

"You got me," she says sweetly.

"The Dark One promised the winner whichever hole he wanted."

"He makes the rules, does he?"

Her voice is different, huskier. I don't hate it.

"I'll let him make this one. I will happily claim a hole, Darling."

Kas comes around an oak tree. He's taken his shirt off and torn a length of fabric from it creating a crude blindfold.

He ties it around her eyes.

"Let it be a surprise," my twin says.

"Maybe this one." I pull at Darling's puffy bottom lip and an excited breath escapes her.

Kas goes behind her and hikes up her dress. "Maybe this one." He gives her bare ass a smack and she yelps, pushing into me where I'm already so hard I could break.

I slide my hand up her thigh and gently graze her pussy. "Or maybe this one." She's dripping fucking wet. Goddamn.

I eye my twin over her shoulder. Technically I won, but I suppose I'm fine with sharing the spoils.

You wanna take her at the same time? I ask my twin.

Stupid question.

I get her mouth, I tell him.

Fine by me.

"On your knees, Darling," I order her and she quickly obeys, falling to the forest floor. There are a lot of exposed, knotted roots in this part of the Neverland woods, so I conjure a soft carpet of moss beneath us and Darling immediately sighs with relief.

I go to the nearest oak tree and sit in a seat among the thick roots. "Get over here, Darling whore."

Blindfold still on, she stays on her hands and knees and crawls to me. I take my cock in the hollow of my fist and give it several pumps as she makes her way to me. My gaze is locked on her mouth, her wet lips and just thinking about burying myself into her throat has my dick swelling in my hand.

When she reaches me, she uses my outstretched legs to guide herself into position. She smells divine, hot and aroused, like a good little slut.

"Open your mouth," I tell her and she drops her jaw. "That's a good girl."

I grip her by a length of her hair and drive her down on me.

As soon as the heat of her mouth is wrapped around me, my eyes slip closed and my hips buck. She drags her tongue up the underside of my shaft, then swirls it around the head, exploring the ridge.

"Fucking hell," I gasp out.

My brother comes up behind her, her ass in the air and when he slides his fingers over her clit, she moans around my dick.

"If I could fuck this tight mouth every fucking day, I would be a happy man." She sinks down the length of me and chokes, comes up for air, then drives back down, her tiny hand wrapped around the base.

The pressure in my balls grows.

Kas gets in between her legs and unzips his pants. Darling hesitates on my dick as she anticipates being filled up by my twin.

"Don't stop, Darling," I tell her. "Don't fucking stop."

She bobs faster and when my brother pushes inside of her wet pussy, she moans loudly.

"Fuck, Darling..." Kas says and thrusts harder, rocking her forward on me.

Her tits bounce against the thin material of her dress, and the friction makes her nipples taut. I graze her, just a tease, and she moans.

Kas reaches around to play with her clit and she pulls up just enough to breathe out roughly around my cock.

"She likes that," I tell him.

"I fucking love that," she says.

"Darling, you're practically dripping down my balls." Kas edges her closer, playing with her sensitive nub.

"Oh god," she moans. "Oh fuck."

"You gonna come for us, Darling?"

"Yes," she says on a breath. "Oh god."

"Don't stop," I tell her, and she takes me into the wet heat of her mouth again stealing away all thought until I am nothing but a rope knotted up desperate to unwind.

"Fuck...fuck Darling..."

Kas shifts his hips, driving into her at an angle and her moans turn into frenzied little mewls as she gets closer and closer to release.

My stomach contracts and my balls tighten and I shove her down my length and spill down her throat. I hold her there, desperate for the final release and the relief that comes from it.

And behind her, my twin pounds into her, filling up her pussy and driving her to her own orgasm.

She moans desperately around my shaft, hips wriggling, body tensing up.

For two brief seconds, I'm flying again amongst the clouds.

For two brief seconds, I can forget that there is such a thing as loss and dying.

Nothing matters but the pleasure of Darling's mouth and the quivering of her own pleasure.

And then her lips pop off my cock and I fall back to earth, disappointed that it's already over.

Kas collapses to the ground on his back and blinks up at the stars, sweat beading on his temple. "Fuck, I needed that."

"Me too." I sink into the crook of the tree.

Darling yanks off her blindfold and rocks back on her knees and drags the back of her hand over her mouth. "I enjoyed tha—"

Hands hook beneath her arms and yank her into the air.

"Hey!" she yells and sails toward the sky.

The Dark One has found her.

20

WINNIE

Flying in the arms of Pan or Vane is like riding a roller coaster to the top of the track and then sailing down the other side. Except with them there is no safety harness.

"Vane!" I shout and wrap my legs around his hips, clinging to him.

"You get fucked, did you Darling?" he asks as the clouds thicken the higher we get.

It's quiet up here in the twilight Neverland sky. Chillier too. But not when I have Vane close.

"The game is the game," I tell him.

He rubs his hardness against my center. "I suppose you're making a mess on me right now, aren't you?"

"Sticky and wet."

He grumbles and then his gaze zeroes in on something behind me and a second later Peter Pan has his chest to my back.

"You found our Darling girl," he says.

"Yeah, getting railed in the forest by two fae princes. Our little slut."

"They made me come," I tell him. "More than you were able to do."

His gaze darkens. "Say that again, Darling."

"They made me come. You didn't."

I know I'm playing with fire. I think I might have lit the match.

Pan yanks my dress off and sends it fluttering to the ocean far below. I make the mistake of watching it go and the obscene height makes me immediately dizzy.

I cling to Vane even harder, the terror very real now.

"Our Darling wants to act like a whore," Vane says, "shall we fuck her like one?"

"We shall."

"Wait," I say.

"No," Pan says.

"We're too high up."

"Then you better hold on to us."

We're so high in the sky now, the clouds are literally floating around us. So close I swear I could reach out and take a handful.

The head of Vane's cock slides up my messy, wet slit, fucking my clit. I'm already buzzing from coming with the twins. I'm so sensitive it makes me jolt and I slip down Vane's hips.

"Don't drop me!"

"Wrap those thighs around me, Darling," Vane orders. "And start fucking."

I lock my arms around his neck and rock up letting his cock find my opening and he sinks in.

Pan gets in close at my backside. "Let's fuck her at the same time."

"You think she can take it?"

"I think she doesn't have a choice."

I moan into Vane's neck.

Pan lines himself up.

"We have to start training her," Vane says. "Loosen her up a bit. This one will hurt, Darling. But I'm sure you know that."

"I can't," I tell them.

"You can," Pan says at my ear.

"I warned you, didn't I Darling?" Vane grabs my chin and forces me to look at him, his two glinting black eyes. "I warned you there'd be punishment."

And then Pan guides his cock into me too and somehow, someway, Peter Pan and the Dark One both fill me up at the same time.

21

WINNIE

THEY WEREN'T LYING. IT HURTS. A LOT. THERE IS A SHARP stinging as they stretch me over both of them, filling me up much more than I have ever been filled up.

But I'm already dripping wet, already full of Kas's cum.

And being mid-air, practically weightless, helps.

Pan grunts as he struggles to seat himself inside of me, but Vane has the better angle and pushes me down the length of him. He's got his hands on my ass, spreading me open for both of them.

"Does it hurt, Darling?" Pan asks on a rasp.

"Yes."

"Do you like being used like a whore?"

"Yes." Heat paints my cheeks admitting it. It may hurt, but there is a tide rising in my belly that I can't deny. A shameful thumping in my chest that I don't want to shake.

I like it.

I like it too much.

And that dark thing inside of me feasts on it.

I can feel its satisfaction just as surely as I could hear the wolf speaking in my head.

Both things are crazy and yet they seem to be true.

Let me in, that voice says.

Let me in.

The breath catches midway up my throat and Vane's eyes narrow as he slows his pace, the look on his face asking and searching.

He can feel it too.

I know he can.

And I think Peter Pan might be right.

I can feel the Dark Shadow like a thousand whirlpools all over my body. An endless churning and a hunger to consume.

Let me in, it says again in the far dark corners of my mind. *Let's revel in it as one.*

Okay, I say.

And the darkness rides in.

My nerves are electric. The air is cold, but my skin is hot and my lips pull back in a devilish grin.

Vane's eyes widen. "The fuck?" he says.

"Don't stop," I order him, my voice raspier than it was just a few minutes before.

I sense his shadow reaching out, desperate to connect with something like itself.

His cock thickens inside of me.

"You have the shadow," he says to me.

"Don't stop," Pan orders. "It'll be better for the shadow if we let her take what she needs."

"Yes, fuck me, Dark One. Make me your cum slut."

Vane growls like he hates my words, but his cock gets even harder, betraying how he feels.

We are all creatures of debauchery, debased at the core.

Excitement beats beneath my ribs and some of the pain ebbs away as Pan and Vane turn back to my punishment.

"Yes." I moan and clutch tighter at Vane. "Fuck yes." I hitch my legs higher on his hips and hook my ankles behind him so I can grind against his pelvis as they fuck me together and carry us higher into the dark twilight sky.

"Spread her wider," Pan orders and Vane's grip sinks lower on my ass so he can spread me open.

Pan wraps his hand around my throat and yanks my head back. "Come for us, Darling. Your king commands it."

I shift forward more and find just the right spot to grind my clit against Vane. The pressure builds slower this time. It is that slow ascent of a roller coaster. The pleasure is rising, rising. I pant out a breath, squeeze my eyes shut as Pan and Vane stretch me around their cocks.

"Go on, Win," Vane says with a rumble that reverberates through his chest. "Soak our cocks."

I don't think they're fucking me so much as I'm fucking them now. I get lost in the friction building between me and Vane, the electric pulse at my clit, the power of fucking them both at the same time.

And then the wave chases me, gets closer and closer, all my nerves lighting up.

"Fuck!" I scream as the pleasure crashes over me and Pan and Vane slam into me together, Pan coming, then Vane, both with a loud, animalistic grunt, both filling me up with their cum.

A sharp wind cuts in, cooling some of the sweat on the back of my neck as several quick breaths escape me and the muscles in my arms and legs jerk with the aftershocks.

The dark thing curls away from the surface, sated and I cling to Vane with Pan shielding my backside, keeping the colder twilight air from my nakedness.

Pan is the first to slide out of me and there's a sharp sting as he does and a dull, thudding ache in my pussy.

Vane is next, but I stay locked around him, my face now buried in the crook of his neck.

I don't want to let go.

For one, we're still several hundred feet in the clouds and two...I don't want to let go of *him*.

"Why didn't you tell me?" he says to Pan as he wraps his arm around my waist and pulls me closer, cradling me against him.

The heat of Peter Pan disappears as he flies back. "I just found out."

"Win?" Vane asks.

"She didn't know either," Pan says.

"How did it happen?"

My voice is muffled in his neck as I answer, "I can't remember."

"We should get her back." Pan's voice is fading away. "Get her warm."

"Hold on to me, Win," Vane says.

I keep my arms tightly locked around his neck as he goes parallel with the earth and flies us back to the treehouse.

They all dote on me when we're back together.

Kas gets me clean clothes and a warm sweater. Bash whips up a batch of cloudberry pancakes and then drizzles the stack with fresh maple syrup. I'm stuffing my face with the deliciousness when Vane pours me a drink, but only a shot worth, because apparently it's for "my own good."

Pan makes me a cup of fresh coffee to chase down the alcohol.

It's Pan who fills the twins in on what we've discovered, but I notice he leaves out the part about where I supposedly hurt Vane's brother.

I'm not even going to contemplate having killed him.

There's no way.

Right?

"So Winnie Darling has the Neverland Death Shadow." Bash beams at me. "I'm proud of you, kid."

"No we're not proud of her," Vane argues. "The fucking thing will kill her if we don't get it out."

"It will?" I say, the hot mug of coffee in my hands, warming me up. "It doesn't feel like it would."

"You've been ill since we returned home," Pan points out. "So it's not out of the question that it'll eventually cause you irreparable harm."

And then it dawns on me...

"Smee knew," I say.

The boys all look at me.

"She said something about power and that you all were jackasses because you couldn't see it when it was looking you right in the face. I'm paraphrasing," I add with a smirk.

Pan snorts. "Of course she knew and kept it from me. Fucking Smee."

"It's not like she owes us anything," Kas points out. "She's not technically our ally and we did kidnap her once."

Vane lights a cigarette and takes a long drag on it. After blowing out smoke, he adds, "It was certainly in her best interest to let the Dark Shadow surprise us."

"So how do we get it out?" I ask and as soon as the

question is out of my mouth, I can sense the shadow shaking its head.

Kas runs his fingers through his hair to tie it into a bun. "How did our mother take yours?" he asks Pan. "We were never told the story."

Pan leans against the kitchen counter between Kas and Vane.

God they are gorgeous. Like marble and obsidian carved sharp enough to cut.

I would bleed for them any day.

In the next room, I catch the now familiar sound of wolf nails clicking on the hardwood floor and a second later, the wolf trots in.

"Where have you been?" Bash asks.

"He says he was hunting," I answer.

"Well did he catch anything?" Kas tucks a few loose strands of hair behind his ear.

"Hare, I guess?"

"Good job, Balder." Bash kneels in front of the wolf and gives him a scratch behind the ears.

The wolf practically groans with delight.

"Is Balder his name?" I ask.

Kas pulls himself up on the counter and grabs a handful of leftover berries. "We think so. We had a wolf once named Balder and he—"

The wolf yips and wags his tail.

"Wait," Pan says, his eyes narrowing. "Didn't your wolf end up in the lagoon?"

"He did." Bash straightens and returns to his plate of pancakes, shoveling in a large bite, the muscle in his biceps twining like rope.

"The lagoon returned him?" Pan asks.

"I guess?" Kas pops another berry in his mouth and

then takes one between his fingers and gestures for me to open up. I do, because I like any game, especially with Kas. He aims and then throws the berry and I catch it easily. It's a plump, juicy one and it pops between my teeth.

Vane looks over at Pan. "What is it? I can sense your anxiety."

"I don't like the lagoon bringing things back to life, is all." He pushes away from the counter and goes to the cabinet opposite the kitchen island and pulls out a bottle of scotch. It's so old, the label is handwritten, the paper curling at the edges.

He pops out the cork and takes a drink straight from the bottle.

Vane's frown deepens.

"So how do we remove the Death Shadow from our Darling?" Kas asks.

"Maybe the better question is, how did she get it?" Vane says.

They all look at me, even Peter Pan.

"I...well..."

All of my memories after the pirates in the treehouse are super muddied. But I distinctly remember Cherry asking me for help and then—

Oh no.

"What is it?" Vane comes forward. "You have a look on your face."

Oh no no Cherry!

"Spit it out, Win," Vane says, his bright violet eye searching my face.

I don't want to tell him.

He's going to lose his fucking shit.

I close my eyes and try to conjure the exact memories, the exact words, the exact look on Cherry's face...

She said a bird was stuck in her room and she wanted help getting it out and I was second guessing it because Vane had ordered me into Pan's tomb. But I felt bad for her because I had already taken Vane from her and the twins too.

So I went down to the ground floor and down the hallway to her room and then...

She shoved me inside.

The first edge of the old fear comes back.

The shadow had been darting around the room and I could feel its panic and its hunger.

Then it went still and I could sense it sizing me up.

Then it lunged for me.

"Winnie," Vane says again, this time with more command in his voice.

And that dark thing takes notice. It practically preens for him.

Tell him, it says. *Tell them all the truth. They will kill the girl and they will have proven their loyalty to us.*

I don't want that, I answer.

Don't you?

I can no longer tell if that dark edge of excitement welling in my gut is mine or the shadow's.

"It was Cherry," I answer. "Cherry locked me in a room with it."

22

HOOK

I CAN'T SEEM TO TAKE MY EYES OFF OF HIM.

The fucking Crocodile in my own damn house.

His dark hair is disheveled and it makes him look like the rakish prick he is.

He's still pale from blood loss, but his wounds are already healing.

I always knew he wasn't human. More beast than man.

He is lying in the bed in my guest room, his arm thrown over his middle. He's facing the ceiling so I can see the sharp outline of his profile, the slope of his nose, a slight divot right before the tip.

And then his mouth.

It is a mouth that knows how to bend things to its will.

When I drag my gaze back up, I lurch upright, finding his eyes open.

The wooden chair beneath me lets out a loud squeak and the Crocodile rolls his head my way.

"Captain," he says, his voice thick and hoarse.

I pull my pistol, cock the hammer back and point it at him. I feel better knowing I can put a bullet in him at any moment.

Except he laughs at me. Fucking laughs.

Thankfully the laughter dissolves into a long, dry cough.

"Water, Captain."

"Fuck off."

He smacks his lips together. "Perhaps your blood will do then."

There is nothing I hate more than the sight of my own blood.

And I think he knows it.

I go to the pitcher on the dresser and fill a glass.

With my back to him, the hair along my nape rises and it takes everything I have not to visibly shiver.

"I can hear your heart racing," he says to me.

I grit my teeth and turn back to him, the glass in hand. "I'm excited about the prospect of murdering you."

He snorts and pulls himself upright in the bed, his back against the headboard.

The sheet sloughs off his torso.

Smee removed most of his clothes to get a better look at his wounds.

We had nothing that would fit him once we were finished. The Crocodile is lean around the waist, bulky in the shoulders. My men are lazy and spoiled and pudgy.

I linger in the sight of his firm stomach and the tightly compacted muscle.

He catches me staring and lifts a brow and I shove the water in his face.

"Now start talking." I drop back into the chair.

He brings the glass to his mouth and upends it, drinking back the liquid in three big gulps.

His Adam's apple sinks in his throat and it makes the crocodile mouth tattooed on his neck move like a real mouth.

I swallow hard.

He breathes out with relief when the glass is empty.

I want to murder him.

I will murder him.

Just as soon as I know what's in store for Neverland. There hasn't been outright fighting in a very long time, but anyone worth their salt has likely felt the shift in the wind.

Neverland—the heart of the island—is shaking things up.

Glass still clutched in hand, the Crocodile eyes me.

As enemies, I suppose he wants to hold his secrets close and I sense them there, tucked behind his sharp incisors.

But he's at my mercy, so he must give me something or I'll put a bullet between his eyes.

"Winnie Darling has the Neverland Dark Shadow," he says. "She killed half the Remaldi royal family in a tavern in town. The Remaldis were here to retrieve their shadow from my brother. We were invited by the fae queen who I suspect wants all of the dick on this island dead or subservient, including yours."

Well...that was more than I bargained for. More than I thought he'd give me.

Do I believe it?

Say what you will about the Crocodile—he may be brutal, remorseless, and cruel, but he doesn't strike me as a liar.

Too much pride for that.

So a Darling has the shadow? How the hell did that happen?

"Why did they fight you?" I ask him. "Do you not hold more allegiance to Vane than you do the royals?"

His teeth grit together and he shows the first hint of emotion since he arrived on my doorstep.

"The princess was mine," he says. "And the Darling killed her."

I snort. "You don't have the capacity to love, beast."

"Did I say 'love', Captain? I said she was mine. There's a difference."

My arm aches just below the wrist where my hook takes over.

That old, festering wound, the one that you cannot see, the one that is a ghost of memory and pain, throbs again.

"Is that what she was to you? A possession?" I hold my hook up. "Is that why you took my hand? Because I touched your *property*?"

"Why else?" he asks.

I run my tongue along the inside of my bottom lip, debating where I should inflict the deadly wound. In the gut would cause him the most pain. But the dick would make him howl.

"I knew you didn't love her. She was too good for you. You just wanted to possess the pretty Darling girl and debase her with your filth."

He laughs and shakes his head. "You saw in Wendy Darling what she wanted you to see. And that is why I liked her. Because she was smart enough to know it and cutthroat enough to make you believe it."

The festering wound transmutes to anger and before I can think better of it, I'm lunging at him.

The sharp tine of my hook presses against his throat

where his beating heart pulses beneath the pale skin. He sits perfectly still.

"Say that one more time and I'm tearing out your throat."

He smiles up at me. "You could try." He sneaks in beneath my guard, bringing his foot to my sternum and shoving me back.

I catch myself on the dresser and the pitcher of water teeters on its bottom.

The Crocodile gets out of bed and his trousers, now without his belt, slouch low on his hips.

"You are an uncivilized beast."

"You think this is beastly, just wait until my time runs out."

"The fuck does that mean?"

"I don't know, Captain. Where's my clock? Fetch it and I'll tell you how long you have before you find out."

"I don't have your clock. And if you arrived with one, I would have smashed it to pieces."

I have hated the sound of a ticking clock ever since he took my hand.

He looks toward the open window. "Well that's not good."

"What? What's not good?"

"Give me your blood, Captain."

"Absolutely not."

"It's better if you volunteer it."

I pull my pistol again and grow weary with this back and forth. I should just kill him now, be done with it. My nightmare would be over and I could finally move on.

The hammer clicks as I lock it back.

"I wouldn't, Captain," he warns.

"Or what?"

He darts forward. I pull the trigger. The pistol lets out a loud KAPOW and the lead ball hits the window casing across the room.

The Crocodile barrels into me. We slam against the wall together and my pistol slips from my grip as he pins me in place.

"You were really going to shoot me?" he asks, a smile lifting the corner of his mouth.

"As if there is any question that I want you dead."

I knee him in the balls.

The air rushes out of him and he sinks to the floor, his face going red.

"Christ, Captain," he says, his voice stilted. "If you wanted me on my knees, all you had to do was ask."

"Will you shut up?"

"I don't prefer it," he answers.

Smee comes running into the room, looks at the Crocodile, then at me. "What happened?"

I run my hand through my hair, smoothing it over. "A disagreement."

"I need blood," the Crocodile says. "Smee, you know a thing or two about that, don't you?"

I look over at her, hoping to spot the abject disbelief at being roped into his ruse. But there is no such thing on Smee's face.

"You know what he is?"

"I know of what he might be."

"And you didn't tell me?!"

"It was a working theory, Jas." Smee steps back into the hall and calls for one of the pirates. It's Daniel who comes shuffling down the hall. He's half drunk and half asleep.

Smee points to the Crocodile. "Give him your wrist."

"I prefer them sober," the Crocodile says.

"This isn't a dinner menu," I tell him.

Because Daniel knows better than to argue with orders, he goes to the Crocodile and holds out his arm.

The Crocodile's eyes flash bright yellow.

The shiver that comes over me this time is not one I can contain.

He rises to his feet and towers over Daniel by a handful of inches. When he curls his hands around the pirate's offered forearm, a flame ignites in my gut.

"What is he?" I ask Smee.

"He is a member of the Bone Society, isn't that right?"

The Crocodile drags his tongue over his sharp incisors. "Maybe."

I've heard of the Bone Society and because I hate ticking clocks, I automatically avoid every mention and occurrence of them.

Every clock in the Isles is created by the Society. Every single one.

"Tell him why you have to keep time," Smee coaxes.

The Crocodile gives me a devilish grin, all sharp teeth and shining eyes. "Because when time runs out, if I have yet to have my meal, then I will turn into a beast and devour everything in my path."

"Christ." I lean against the dresser.

"*My* god is time, Captain. Tick, tock. Tick, tock. That is my prayer. Every second. Of every day."

And then he sinks his sharp incisors into Daniel's wrist and drinks his fill.

I can't watch. There is a building in my chest and a heat sinking to my groin that I cannot shake.

Poor form.

Poor form.

I can hear my father's voice echoing in my head. I can no longer conjure an image of his face, but I can still remember the way it felt to be on the other end of his disappointment.

Like I was less than.

Sometimes I wonder if my mother gave birth to me and my father looked down at me swaddled in her arms and said, "Poor form, Elizabeth. Poor form indeed."

I am my own man now. But when I think of my father, I am still a boy constantly failing him.

I go to the bar at the front of the house and pour myself a generous fill of rum.

It burns going down but does nothing for the chill in my veins.

I pour a second and light a cigar and keep it captured between my teeth as I go to the balcony that overlooks the bay.

The moonlight has painted the still water silver. My ship rocks on a wave.

I want to leave.

No, that's not quite right.

I want to *run*.

Instead I sit in one of the hand-carved wooden chairs and balance my glass on the arm.

He finds me several minutes later and lights a cigarette and takes the chair beside me.

"Why keep it at bay?" I ask him. "Why not let it out and destroy Peter Pan on your own if that's what you want? Take your brother home. That's why you're here, isn't it? Maybe you were brought to Neverland by the fae queen and maybe the royals wanted the dark shadow, but you wanted your brother."

"Is that your theory?" He regards me with a pinch of curiosity between his dark brows.

I say nothing and he says nothing and that says everything.

I realize he and I have more in common than I might have first guessed. He wants Vane back. I want Cherry. And both of them have chosen others instead of us. Perhaps because we did the same to them once upon a time.

After a stretch of silence, he says, "There is a cost."

A cost to becoming the beast.

"What kind of cost?"

He lays his head back against the wooden chair and turns to me. But the moonlight is at his back so I've lost sight of his face in shadow and goosebumps lift on my arms.

"As if I would tell you my weakness, Captain."

I blow out an exasperated breath. "Very well."

I am acutely aware of the space between us, the space he takes up.

He is my arch nemesis, the reason I have a hook for a hand.

I want him dead.

Do I not?

"If I were you, Captain," he says, "I would bring your sister home. Do not delay."

I roll the cigar around my tongue, savoring the sweet tobacco.

"Did you see her?" I ask.

"I did."

"And?"

"And something is wrong with her."

I lurch forward. “What do you mean?”

“Beasts can sense fear and she is terrified of something.”

I’m up on my feet in an instant. “Smee!” I call.

“Captain?”

I pause in the doorway to look back at him.

“Tell Smee to be wary of my brother. Tell her to be wary of them all.”

23

CHERRY

My bag is packed.

There's no sense even saying goodbye. None of them will miss me, after all.

I take one more look around my room. There is nothing here that is a representation of me. I think it's been so long since I had something that was mine that I can't quite put my finger on who I am beyond my brother and the Lost Boys.

I don't want to leave the treehouse and the thought of finally letting go of Vane makes me want to puke, but there is nothing left for me here.

And I don't know if there's anything left for me on Neverland.

I flick off the light and leave the room and pull the door closed behind me. Down the hall, a dark shadow blocks out the golden glow of the light in the foyer and I know it's Vane even though I can't make out his face.

I know him because I would know him anywhere.

And because my body is reckless and stupid, my stomach fills with butterflies and my heart leaps to my throat.

My heart is excited to see him. My brain is yelling RUN.

The first thread of terror ribbons around my ribs.

"Vane," I start, but when he passes through a spot of light cast by one of the sconces, I see the look on his face and I know...I *know*.

He's on me in a second and he takes me by the hair and yanks me down the hallway.

Pain lances through my scalp. I stumble over my own feet trying to keep up with him.

"Vane, please," I beg even though he hasn't said a word.

Through the foyer, he goes to the front door and whips it open. It bangs against the wall.

The others watch from the winding staircase. None of them stop Vane. None of them care.

Maybe they never did.

It makes me feel worthless.

Before Vane can get me over the threshold, I trip, caught up in my own panic and I slam down to my butt.

I'm facing the stairwell now, my hair twisted around in Vane's grip and I lock eyes with Winnie at the top of the stairs. There's no hint of what she's thinking, no hint of the shadow holding her hostage.

But I know they all know.

There's no talking my way out of this one.

"I didn't mean to," I say, my voice cracking as Vane drags me across the wide threshold and then down the steps, each straight edge banging against my hip. I hold on to his wrist trying to take some of the pressure off my hair.

When I hit the ground, dirt puffs up around us and grits between my teeth.

The gravel crunches beneath his boots as it scrapes my skin raw.

I try to get my feet beneath me, but it's no use. He's impatient and far too strong to fight.

A dull ache thuds in my head as several chunks of hair tear loose.

When he reaches the fork in the pathway, he drops me, steps back and points his head toward the twilight sky, eyes closed. He takes a deep breath.

Blood is starting to well in the scrapes along my calves, but the pain is distant now as the fear takes over and adrenaline pumps through my veins.

I scramble to my feet. Tears blur my vision, turning Vane into a dark smudge against the night. "You have to believe me. I didn't know what would happen."

I'm not lying, exactly.

I didn't know the shadow would take hold in Winnie. I thought it would kill her. Which is so much worse.

And I think he knows exactly what I intended.

And I think I've never seen him as angry as he is now.

My stomach churns and all of the butterflies are gone.

With a grit of his teeth, Vane pulls out a cigarette, puts the dark filter between his lips. His lighter flashes beneath the moonlight a second later and the lid clicks open.

The flame paints him in sharp gold as he brings the end to the cigarette and inhales.

He closes the lighter with a definitive snap.

He's angry with me and I want him to love me and I don't know how to undo this.

Stupid Winnie.

Why did she have to...well...be so damn likable?

Even now, I don't want to hate her. I wanted her to be my friend. I wanted to belong. I wanted...

My chin wobbles with the threat of tears.

I wanted Vane to love me more than anything in the world.

Winnie has him and I don't.

In the woods, the wolves are yipping and the crickets are chirping and here at the fork in the path, my body is trembling.

Vane pulls the cigarette away and exhales a breath of smoke.

"I'm sorry," I say again, but my voice is barely above a whisper.

"I know you are, Cherry."

My heart breaks hearing the regret in his voice.

"I didn't...I mean..."

He takes another hit from the cigarette and watches me with his mismatched eyes.

"Tell me what to do. I'll do it. Just please—" I reach out for him and he pivots away.

"You want to know what to do?" The cigarette hangs at his side, clipped between his fingers, glowing in the dark. The night smells of honeysuckle and burning tobacco and Vane.

Tell me what to do.

I'm desperate for his forgiveness and I'll do fucking anything.

"Start running," he says.

I gulp down a breath and stagger back as his violet eye goes black and his hair turns white.

"Start running, Cherry. Because I'm going to fucking kill you."

24

CHERRY

I START RUNNING.

There's nothing else to do *but* run.

But I'm not built to run faster than the Dark One and I sure as hell can't fight him.

I follow the path away from the house, my heart hammering so hard in my ears, my ear drums are ringing.

I can hear his footsteps behind me.

His terror, the Death Shadow's terror, washes through me like poison. It makes me feel sick and desperate and so fucking alone.

I can't outrun him.

Will it hurt when he kills me?

I reach the main road and turn toward James's territory, toward the only place I can call home.

And just as I round the corner where the path forks, a shadow comes racing toward me.

My brain isn't working—it's too full of adrenaline to make out what it is.

But the voice that yells at me is one I know.

"Duck!" Smee shouts.

She veers sharply to the side of the road, her pace at full speed, and jumps at a large boulder, propelling herself into the air.

I skid on the gravel and slam to the ground as she sails over top of me, her dagger drawn, clutched in hand, the blade glinting in the moonlight.

Rolling to my knees, I turn at the last second and watch as she drives the blade through Vane's chest.

The sickening crack of a bone breaking rents through the night.

"No!" I scream and scramble to my feet. "Smee, no!"

Vane's eyes are black, his hair white, but there is pain etched into his face as he wraps his hands around the blade, blood pouring from his palms and his chest.

"She's someone's *sister*," Smee says and leans into the hilt, sinking the blade deeper.

In the dark, several etchings on the blade pulse with light.

"You knew better, Dark One," Smee adds as he chokes on blood.

"Smee, please," I grab for her arm. "Please don't kill him."

She looks over at me.

"*Please.*"

She yanks the blade out as the others appear at the top of the hill.

"Vane!" Winnie screams.

Smee ignores the blood dripping from her sword and rams it back into its sheath. "Go," she tells me and shoves me down the road, keeping herself between me and the rest of them.

I start moving, but I can't help but watch Vane over my shoulder as I stagger away.

The blood pouring out of him and the surprise on his face.

The Dark One thought he was invincible.

I think we all thought so too.

He drops to his knees, clutching at his chest and though he just tried to hunt me down like an animal, I can't shake the fear that he might die and this is the way he will see me last—a terrified girl who betrayed him and then left him for dead.

I want to help him, but I think I'm the last person he wants at his side.

I can almost feel his repulsion.

"Go!" Smee yells again and shoves me.

This time, I run and don't look back.

25

KAS

"Get him up!" Pan screams.

I hook one of Vane's arms around my shoulder while Pan takes the other. Vane is practically dead weight and he can barely get his feet beneath him.

Blood is fucking everywhere.

"Vane!" Darling screams again and Bash hooks into her, yanking her back, trying to keep her from slowing us down.

The air smells of violence and regret.

We get him in the house and up the stairs to the loft and drop him on the sofa.

He's listless and pale. His arm drops from his side as his eyes roll back in his head.

"Fix him," Darling says. She has her tiny hands fisted in Bash's shirt. "Fix him!"

"We're trying, Darling," my brother says. "Calm down."

"Calm down? *Calm down*?!" She comes over to the sofa and hangs over the back. "Can't he heal? Why is he so pale? Why isn't he healing?"

Pan tears off Vane's shirt to reveal a large, gaping wound just below his heart. "Rags," he orders. "Wet ones. Now."

I race to the kitchen, my hands on autopilot.

Why the fuck isn't he healing?

Out of everyone on the island, I suppose Smee is the one who might know how to defeat the Dark One. But why the hell would she wait until now to do it?

We promised her we would bring Cherry back and we lied.

Oath breakers, the lot of us.

If Smee had been a few minutes later…

Or earlier for that matter.

Which begs the question why she was there at all.

When I come back out to the loft, Vane's breathing is labored. Darling is sitting on the floor beside him, his hand in hers, her eyes glassy with unshed tears.

"Vane," Pan says and smacks him. "Come on, wake up."

I hand my brother one of the wet rags and we get to work cleaning the wound so we can see what we're dealing with.

Nani taught us a lot about healing, but our medicinal work revolved around the fae. Salve was Nani's favorite cure, but I'm not sure a bit of faerie goop will heal this wound.

Bash and I both look at one another when we see the state of things.

The wound is edged in black and there's something dark leaking out of him, something other than blood.

If I didn't know any better, I'd say it was the Death Shadow. It's airy like ocean spray but dark like shadow.

That can't be good, Bash says.

I know.

"Hey," Pan says and snaps his fingers at us. "You talk to me. You tell me what's going on."

"Honestly?" Bash sits back on his butt on the floor. "This is unprecedented, even for us."

"You've got the shadow," Darling says to Pan. "Can't you heal him?"

"It doesn't work like that." He looks down at Vane sprawled on the couch. "Besides, I can feel his shadow pushing me away."

Darling brings Vane's hand to her mouth and presses a gentle kiss to his bloody knuckles as the tears finally spill over her lids. "Then what do we do?"

My twin meets my gaze behind Pan's back. *Can The Dark One die?*

Anything can die. Even Peter Pan.

Pan and Darling aren't going to let him go so easily, Bash says.

And neither are we.

Behind us, Balder trots into the room. He comes up behind Darling and curls into her, resting his chin on her shoulder. A soft whine sounds in the back of his throat and Darling cries harder.

"We're going to fix him, Darling," Pan says as he wipes away one of her tears. "You hear me?"

"Do you promise?"

Pan hesitates before he answers. Even he must know he can't promise this.

But he nods anyway, because I think he needs to believe it just as much as Darling does.

None of us want Vane to die.

I think I'm coming to realize we would all die for one another.

When did that happen?

When did I suddenly feel more loyalty and allegiance to this disparate found family than I did my own flesh and blood?

I feel the rightness of it though, thumping like a wild thing in the center of my chest.

Balder lifts his head and looks right at me and blinks at me with his bright blue eyes.

You find what you need when you need it.

Nani used to love saying that to us when we were boys and I'm not sure if I'm just conjuring her words or if Balder is actually reciting them in my head.

And the island gives you what you need when you need it.

I look at the wolf again. The resemblance to the original Balder is uncanny. I didn't want to believe that it was really him, that the island could do something so profound as bring someone back to life.

And yet here he is.

Balder's tail thumps loudly behind him.

"Get him to the lagoon," I say.

Pan looks at me.

"The lagoon. Now."

Winnie lurches upright. "Yes. He loves the lagoon and the lagoon loves Vane. You said it yourself, Pan, the waters can be healing."

"Yes but they can be fickle too. Ask the twins."

Bash and I shrug. "At this point, it's worth the risk, isn't it?" Bash says.

Pan sits back on his butt and drapes his arm over his upturned knee, thinking.

He must know we're running out of options.

But he's always been wary of the lagoon.

"Fine." Pan grumbles. "Get him up again."

This time, Bash and I each take one of Vane's arms and

hook them around our shoulders. He's completely out now and there's no helping us so his legs drag as we make our way out of the house and through the woods and down the dirt path.

Rain starts to spit from the sky and by the time we get Vane down to the beach, thick, fat drops are falling from dark, swirling clouds.

It's almost like the island is matching our somber mood.

When we reach the water's edge, Bash and I move to drag him in, but Darling stops us.

"I'll take him," she says and when I glance at her over my shoulder, darkness is writhing around her eyes, just itching to take over.

"Darling," Pan says, "I don't think that's such a—"

"I'll take him, Pan. It has to be me."

There is new determination in her voice. She's not just our naughty, bold Darling. She's something else now, something that does not back down even when standing against Peter Pan.

"All right." Pan finally relents and steps back. "We'll be right here if you need us."

She comes in close to me and wiggles in under Vane's arm, taking his weight.

Despite the fact he's like twice her size, she barely droops beneath the new burden.

Bash unhooks Vane's arm from around his shoulder and says, "You good, Darling?"

"I'm good." She keeps her arm hooked around Vane's waist and drags him into the water.

26

ROC

I don't like underestimating people and I suspect I've underestimated far too many since landing on Neverland.

I underestimated Peter Pan and Vane and the new Darling.

James is still up in the air.

He's pacing the barroom, his right hand clamped over his left wrist behind his back, his hook sticking out behind him.

In almost every room, there is a worn path on the hardwood floor where the varnish has worn off. The Captain likes to pace, it would seem.

I crack a peanut shell and pop the innards into my mouth. "Will you sit down?"

"I don't think when I'm sitting."

"I can't think when you're pacing."

He stops in the middle of the room and furrows his brow over his green eyes. "What do you have to think about?"

"Strategy, Captain. Because we need one. Like now."

On a breath, he spins and resumes his course. "You said the Remaldi royals were working with the fae queen? So we need to pick a side—"

"I am never on a side." I pop another peanut into my mouth and crunch it between my molars. "There is only my side."

He scoffs at me and waves his hook in the air. "You're ridiculous and you're not helping."

"Mmm well, you're wasting time. Any minute Holt will come knocking on your door, maybe even with the fae queen in tow, and so you'll have to know what you plan to say to them. The fae queen will eventually want you dead. Or subservient and while I think you'd wear submission quite well" —the glare he shoots me could roast a chicken — "I suspect being the fae queen's puppet will not. And Holt will just want to use you and your men as cannon fodder, since the Darling took out several of his."

I drop the cracked shells of several peanuts into an empty glass on the bartop, then dust off my pants. "Tell me, Captain, what is your preferred outcome?"

He looks at me over his shoulder as he paces to the windows. "I want you dead, Peter Pan dead, and Smee and Cherry safely returned here."

"Well, you'll probably get two out of four, so your odds aren't bad."

"I *will* kill you," he promises.

"I'm sure you will." I flash him my innocent smile, but I keep my chin up so he can get a good look at the crocodile teeth tattooed on my flesh.

He snorts and comes back around. I head him off between two round tables.

We are not much different in height, but he's wearing

bulkier clothes than I am, all pomp and circumstance with this one. I like it. There's something about James that reminds me of a crust of dirt on a beautiful vintage timepiece. I want to lick my thumb and smudge it off and see how he gleams beneath.

"If we drew a Venn diagram of your preferred outcome and my preferred outcome, we would have a nice overlapping center," I tell him.

A wrinkle appears between his brows and his eyes search mine looking for the catch. "Which is what?"

"Peter Pan dead."

"Why do you want him dead?"

"I have my reasons."

I could tell him about Wendy. It would motivate him even more. But I haven't decided if I want to compete with him yet.

I am a greedy fuck, after all. And what's mine is mine.

But I think the feud between Pan and Hook has been going on just long enough he doesn't really need a sensible reason anymore. History is reason enough.

James isn't a strategist. He thinks he is. But he's been misusing his strengths. James has a knack for motivating people to his cause, even if it's a shitty one.

If he would stop fucking around and use that power, instead of chasing demons, he might shift earth.

"How about we team up and kill Peter Pan together?"

"He's unkillable," he says, but I can hear the desire in his voice for that to be untrue.

"Or maybe no one has used the right weapon."

There is the slightest uptick at the corner of his mouth. I can't help but sink my gaze to it, to the way his lips curve over one another. A tasty fucking snack.

"You have such a weapon?" he asks.

I give him a light slap to the cheek and he growls in the base of his throat.

"You're looking at it, Captain. I am, after all, the Devourer of Men."

Smee returns with Cherry. Both are covered in blood.

I don't need confirmation from her to know whose blood it is.

I would recognize my brother's scent anywhere.

"What happened?" James asks.

"I stabbed Vane," Smee answers and goes around behind the bar to pour herself a drink.

Keeping my expression blank, my emotions indiscernible, I ask, "And how did you manage that?"

"She has a magical sword." Cherry's voice wavers. There are wet streaks in the dirt on her freckled face. "I think she killed him." Fresh tears widen the trails.

I grit my teeth. "Did you?"

"No," Smee answers and slings back a shot of apple whisky.

My relief is nearly palpable.

"But he'll need a lot more than a bandage to heal from it," Smee adds.

The pounding in my head is sudden and sharp. I warned my baby brother. Hell, I had planned to teach him a lesson myself. But that was me, this is her.

"Will he die?" I ask her.

She sets her glass down, puts her hands on the bar and leans over it. "He was going to kill Cherry."

"They promised to return her!" the Captain shouts.

"It's my fault." Cherry's voice wobbles and she drags her hand beneath her nose. "It was all my fault."

"What was?" her brother asks.

"Winnie. I cornered her in a room with the Neverland Death Shadow and somehow it got into her."

Well that's definitely not how I thought that had gone down.

"Points to you, Cherry Girl. That was bold."

She rakes her teeth over her bottom lip and shakes her head.

"Bloody hell." James scratches at the back of his head. "That complicates things."

"No, it doesn't." It does. "It'll make defeating Peter Pan even easier." It won't.

"How do you figure?"

"I saw the Darling in town, remember? She doesn't have control of the shadow. It'll be the distraction we need."

Dubious at best.

But really, I work better when I'm winging it.

"You'll never get to him," Cherry says and we all look at her. "Peter Pan. But Winnie and Vane are his weaknesses. If you want to know how to get to him." And then she turns and leaves the room.

"Looks like your sister is already proving to be an advantage."

James takes a step like he means to go after her but pauses before he does. "Let's set up a meeting with the royals. The fae and the Darklands. Let's be done with Peter Pan once and for all."

When he's gone, I return to my peanuts. I'm fucking starving. The little taste of pirate blood was not enough. Not even close.

Smee pours herself another drink and swirls the liquor around in the glass.

"I have a question, Smee. Something that's been bothering me."

Her tongue pokes at the inside of her cheek. "Answers cost you a pound sterling."

I reach into my pocket and produce a coin and flick it across the bar to her. She snatches it easily from the air, but then looks at it in her open palm.

"Go on," she says.

"Did you know Wendy Darling was pregnant when she left Neverland?"

She pokes again at her cheek, but then runs her tongue along her bottom teeth.

The second coin rings out when I send it sailing down the length of the bar toward her and it hits an abandoned glass.

"Did you know she was on Everland?"

Her gaze meets mine.

"You are widely traveled in the Isles and you have birds everywhere. Of course you knew."

She straightens, sets the glass aside.

"Does James know there is a Darling girl on the other side of the island that is his great-great–"

Smee reaches across the polished bar top to clamp her hand over my mouth. "Don't."

Brave woman, getting near the sharp teeth of a crocodile.

Gently, I take her by the wrist and pull her hand away. "Do you plan to tell him?"

"Why do you care?"

"Answers cost a pound sterling." I smile at her. She rolls her eyes spectacularly and yanks her hand from my grip.

"Why didn't you get her out?" I ask. "Why not tell him?"

"Wendy Darling was in an Everland prison. The obstacles and complexities of breaking her out were insurmountable and she was not my mess to clean up. And despite what people say about James, his heart might be the biggest on all of Neverland. He cares, *deeply*, and if I'd told him about Wendy, he would have gone after her, and then he'd either be dead, or fighting two wars on two islands when the war he already had was already costing him more than he could afford.

"Furthermore, what do you think Peter Pan would have done if he realized the Darling line was now a Hook line? The best-case scenario was to rescue the baby and return it to its world."

"So did you?"

I may be James's enemy, and James may be one of Smee's closest friends, but I'm not Smee's enemy and Smee is not one to hold grudges. She is a woman of action and she's always strategizing.

I suspect she's at least half the reason James has been able to get by all these years without getting his dick chopped off.

I can practically see the wheels turning in her gaze now.

Smee is a walking, talking chessboard and I do love chess.

"I did rescue the baby," she admits.

"To perpetuate the legacy of Peter Pan and the Darlings?"

"To keep the status quo," she answers. "And because moving that baby to the mortal realm was the safest place for it to be. I promised Wendy I would hide her daughter and I did. But Peter Pan still found her. Unfortunately, I underestimated his ability to find a Darling."

"But you've been checking up on the Darlings all along, haven't you." It's not a question.

"I did what I could."

I nod and crack open another peanut. "I wouldn't tell him."

"Why not?"

"Because he'll be angry with you, and then he'll go after her and then I'd have to kill him."

I pop the peanut in my mouth, crush it between my teeth and give her a wink.

She scowls at me.

I think if Smee could, she'd be stabbing me next.

HOOK

It doesn't take much to locate Cherry.

I find her in her old room scanning the pictures tacked up on her wall. She used to love cutting pictures out of the illustrated fairytales and homemaking books.

"You left everything the way it was," she says when she spots me in the doorway.

"Of course."

She makes a turn around the room.

When I built this house, I let her pick which room she wanted. She went with one on the lower level, far away from the pirates and the drinking and cavorting. I was glad she did.

I had never intended to bring her on this trip. The one fateful trip that saw a wrong turn somewhere, landing us in the Isles.

I had meant to sail to the Caribbean.

I never made it.

When I discovered Cherry hiding in the ship's hold, I

had a thought to turn around and return her home. But then I remembered why I was leaving, why I was so desperate to escape.

I couldn't leave her alone with our father.

Cherry sits on her bed now and a cloud of dust kicks up. She waves it away. The sun isn't up yet so there is only the amber glow of the glass sconces on the wall.

I sit beside her and try to search the vastness of my guilt and my shame for an apology that doesn't sound contrite.

She leans her head against my shoulder and there is a stinging deep in my sinuses.

I take her hand in mine.

"Why do we continue to love those who hate us, Jas?" she asks.

I think she means to speak of Vane, but we both hear the unsaid name—Commander William H. Hook. Our father.

When I was a young man, I hated him and yet wanted his admiration in equal measure. I can still hear his voice in my head on frequent occasions telling me when I've fucked up.

Cherry didn't get the worst of our father, but she didn't get the best either.

"I don't know," I answer and give her hand a squeeze. "Gluttons for punishment, it would seem."

One night, in late November, a very long time ago, our father caught me in the stables with one of the servants. "You are an embarrassment!" he shouted and whipped me with his belt. "A shame on this house." Then he kicked me in the ribs and kept kicking until my ribs cracked.

I can still see Cherry huddled under the table wincing and trembling with each hit.

She was never meant to witness the violence and yet somehow it keeps finding her.

Not that she turned her head and pretended not to see.

Three days later, I caught her drugging father's brandy.

Father was in and out of consciousness for seven days.

It was arguably the quietest, most restful stretch of our early lives.

"I want to go home, Jas," she says now.

"Our home no longer exists."

"I don't care where it is or what it looks like. I want to go home."

I think I understand what she's asking for—a stable place and a place to be loved.

"I'll find you a home," I tell her. "A big brother promise to make up for my past transgressions."

She looks up at me with her big, wide eyes. She has our mother's freckles and more of our mother's red hair.

Cherry barely remembers her, but I do.

She too loved someone who hated her.

Maybe that is our legacy. A maddening one at that.

"Don't break this promise," she tells me. "I will never forgive you."

I lean over and plant a kiss atop her head. "I won't."

28

ROC

WHEN HOLT SHOWS UP AT HOOK'S HOUSE, HE'S DAMP FROM THE rain and not the good kind of damp. He's surrounded by the remainder of his guard, which is not many. Matthieu is by his side.

The younger Remaldi cousin looks like he might have had one too many sniffs of everpowder, but who am I to judge?

When Holt spots me in the barroom, he charges at me, dagger out, then slams me into the wall and places the blade at the pulse point in my throat.

"You fucking traitor." His eyes are bloodshot. Was he crying or is he sleep-deprived? He always wanted the throne and now he has it by right. He should be thanking me. Not that I had anything to do with his sister's death.

"If you'll kindly remove your blade," I tell him.

"Or you'll what?" A vein throbs on his forehead.

"Or I'll eat you."

His nostrils flare. He can't tell if I'm joking. I'm not.

The pressure disappears and he staggers back.

I straighten my borrowed shirt. "Holt, if you want to win back your shadow and secure your throne, stop acting like a jilted little boy and start acting like a king."

The fae queen's wings flutter behind her as she watches the room.

What was it I said about underestimating everyone on Neverland? I may have done the same with her.

She's tenacious. And possibly more observant than reckless.

She's been fighting Peter Pan just as long as Hook. But neither have won. Proof is harder to ignore.

"If you'll have a seat," James says and nods at one of the round tables.

Several of his pirates are dotted around the room, several at each entrance and exit. They seem to have varying degrees of capabilities unlike the fae queen's warriors who aren't quite sure if they showed up for war or an early breakfast.

The queen must be having doubts. She's ill-equipped for this war and that's becoming glaringly obvious with every passing day.

She reminds me a bit of Giselle. A woman in power who has to work twice as hard as the men to keep it.

The question is, does she deserve to keep it?

Holt gives the hem of his tunic a sharp yank and then takes a seat. Matthieu stays standing just behind him.

James sits across from him, then the fae queen joins them.

Smee and I take the remaining seats next to one another. She brings with her the scent of her cigarillos, a bit of sweetness and earthiness.

"Vane has been wounded," Hook says, and Tilly and

Holt's expressions immediately shift, registering the surprise and shock.

"How?" Holt asks.

"Not important," James says. "If you want your shadow back, now is the time to strike."

"And James and I plan to help you deal with Peter Pan under one condition."

The Captain glares at me. I can practically see the steam shooting out his ears because we never discussed a condition.

"What is it?" the fae queen asks.

"We'll help you, but my brother is left unharmed."

Holt leans back in his chair and puffs out his chest. "Vane is prone to revenge. We all know that."

"Yes, and his streak of revenge was directly connected to our sister and the Lorne family. Not you and yours."

I'm not entirely sure how my brother will react to having the shadow taken from him, but that's another problem for another day.

One of the pirates brings over several glasses and an uncorked bottle of rum. He sets a glass in front of each of us and fills them with a few fingers of liquor.

"All right," Holt finally says and takes the offered drink in hand. "James, you'll lend us your men?"

James's gaze immediately cuts to mine. I lift a brow. *See*? my brow says.

"I can spare a few," he answers.

"I would also like my brothers to remain unharmed," Tilly adds. "Let me deal with them."

Holt nods once. "As you wish."

James downs his liquor. He barely winces at the burn. "The next question is, where do we stage this coup?"

"The treehouse would be a risk," Smee says.

"I agree," James says.

"Perhaps we could lure them—" Holt starts, but Cherry appears in the doorway and cuts him off.

"If Vane is injured, they'll take him to the lagoon. That's where they'll be."

I'm shocked she'd give him up so easily.

Maybe he betrayed her one too many times.

"Then it's settled." Holt shoves his chair back. "We should leave now and take them by surprise."

"I agree." I down my rum and stand next to him, giving him my most irreproachable smile. "I hope your magic rock does its job."

Holt reaches for it hanging from the end of the chain. "Of course it will."

Honestly, I'm hoping it works. Because if he does manage to take the shadow from my brother, I plan to take it from Holt.

And it'll be much easier to steal as a magic rock than as a shadow.

I smile at Holt and gesture for the door. "After you, Your Highness."

I'm going to enjoy watching that mother fucker die.

29

WINNIE

We've been floating in the lagoon for what feels like hours, just me and Vane. The rain has stopped and the dark clouds have thinned letting some of the remaining twilight to shine above.

Vane is conscious again, which is better than when we arrived, but his breathing is labored and every handful of minutes, his body jolts and the shadow tries leaving his body through the gaping wound in his chest.

"Why isn't this working?" I call to the others.

Pan is sitting beside the wolf, absently scratching at his neck while Bash and Kas play catch with a large seed pod.

"Give it time," Kas calls. "The lagoon can be picky about how and when it gives up its magic."

"Darling," Vane says, his voice weak. "You should go."

"I'm not leaving you." I swim closer to him. He's on his back, the waterline undulating around his body. "Do you feel any better?"

He grits his teeth at a fresh wave of pain and black mist

kicks up from the festering wound. I can barely stand to look at it, it's so bad.

"I think it's getting worse."

When the panic rises again in my throat, I quickly swallow it back down.

"Maybe you need to ask the lagoon for help."

He snorts. "If begging is required, I'll fucking die."

"Don't you dare say that."

"I can feel the shadow wanting to leave." He lifts his head just enough to look over at me. "And when it does, I'm not sure what will be left."

"You still haven't told me what you are beyond the shadow..."

His teeth chatter. "There's a reason my brother is known as the Crocodile. I'm no different." He gets his legs beneath him and treads water slowly. "There was a time I thought getting rid of the shadow would be best. That I could control who I was a lot easier than I could control the shadow. But the more I'm around you, the more..." He trails off and rolls again to his back.

"You what?" I coax.

"I am a monster either way. You would be better off without me."

"I swear to fucking god, if you keep talking like that I will..."

He gives me the joy of laughing this time. "You'll what?"

"Make you take me out for brunch in my world."

"Brunch?" He says the word like it tastes bitter. "The fuck is brunch?"

"The meal between breakfast and lunch?"

"Okay fine. You've talked me into bending to your demands with your threat of ludicrous mortal rituals."

On the shore, the wolf growls.

Peter Pan rises to his feet, his ears turned toward the forest.

Vane swims closer to me. "Do you hear that, Win?"

"Hear what?"

"Heartbeats," he says.

I have barely accepted the fact that I have the Neverland Death Shadow, so whatever power it might have, it's still just out of my reach.

"Listen," Vane whispers.

I close my eyes and turn to my sense of hearing.

And there, just beyond the forest's edge, is the sound of several dozen heart beats.

"Get out of the water!" Pan shouts at us.

"Go." Vane pushes me.

"You're not healed yet!"

"Win, for fuck's sake, listen to me for once!" He shoves me again.

But I barely swim forward a foot before the beach is swarmed.

Fae warriors and pirates and several men dressed in black military uniforms.

And standing at the head of the arrival are Tilly, Captain Hook, the Crocodile, and a man I don't recognize. He's wearing the same style clothing as the queen in the tavern so I guess he must be the royal family who arrived to take Vane's shadow.

"Fucking Roc," Vane says at my ear.

I have a vague recollection of meeting Roc already. I also have a vague memory of killing him.

Or so I thought.

"Is he that much of an asshole?" I ask Vane. "Why is he siding with them?"

Vane shakes his head. "Sometimes it's hard to figure out what the fuck he's thinking."

Peter Pan faces off with the small army. "I don't know what you think your plan is, but it's ill-advised."

The twins flank him. Bash says, "Dear sister, is this really what you want your legacy to be?"

"Don't pretend like you wouldn't be doing the same thing if your kingdom was in jeopardy," the queen says. "We all know the Darling has the shadow and we all know she lost control in town and murdered several innocent people."

Pan snorts. "Giselle was hardly innocent."

"Amara was."

The crowd shifts its attention to Roc at the end of the line. He's got a cigarette in his mouth, one eye squinted to keep the sting away from the smoke ribboning around his face.

I know I did what they all say I did. But I'm not that person.

Aren't you?

The dark energy slithers in my gut.

"Get them out of the water," Tilly orders.

Her fae soldiers take to the air, wings beating so fast, they turn iridescent as they reflect the light of the moon.

"Tilly," Kas says, "I swear to our gods, if you—"

But she doesn't wait for the threat.

Instead she flicks her wrist and the entire beach starts to undulate like it's a living thing.

Kas and Bash spread out their arms to try to keep their balance. Pan takes to the air.

The fae soldiers dart across the surface of the lagoon, not quite touching the water.

"Time to go," Vane says and wraps his arm around my waist from behind.

"Where?"

I barely get the question out before Vane is yanking us from the water. The beach grows smaller and smaller the higher up we go.

And although I've been into the air a few times now, my very mortal brain doesn't like it one bit.

My cry of surprise echoes across the lagoon.

Vane's flight path veers sharply to the right and then we're suddenly crashing to the ground.

When we hit the sloped side of Marooner's Rock, a jolt of pain shoots up my thighs. Vane loses his grip and we both tumble down the mossy rock.

I slam to a halt against the backside of a boulder. Vane is several feet away on his back gasping for air. More black mist trails from his open wound.

"Why did you do that?" I scurry over the rock to him. His next inhale is wet and shallow. "Vane, goddammit!" He rolls to all fours, collapses, then falls to his side. There's a vacant look in his violet eye.

The fae soldiers are not far behind us. Down below on the beach, I can hear the sound of blades clashing and people shouting.

Come on Death Shadow. You came out and wreaked havoc once before. I need your magical madness once again.

I'm greeted with complete and utter silence.

You can't be serious!

"Win," Vane says.

The soldiers are going to be on us in seconds.

I hook Vane's arm around my shoulder and grunt as I

leverage us up. Blood from his open wound soaks my shirt, but it's thick and dark, not the bright crimson blood should be. "We'll jump off the rock," I tell him. "Go to my world to hide you. I'll come back and help them—" I drag him to the cliff's side and he digs in his boots.

"You don't know the first thing about portal jumping," he says with a grumble.

"Sure I do. You go to the cliff. Jump. Easy peasy."

"Says the girl who is always terrified to jump. That and you're on the wrong side."

Ocean spray glitters in the moonlight.

"There is no portal at the bottom on this side. You jump from here, you'll be impaled on the rocks below."

With him still listing at my side, I ease to the edge of the cliff and peer over. Craggy, sharp rocks break through the surf several hundred feet below.

Okay maybe I don't know what I'm doing.

"So what's your bright idea?" I ask.

He unhooks his arm from around me and stumbles forward. "You'll fly away and I'll face them alone."

"Hah!"

He may be on death's door, but he's apparently still capable of scowling at me.

"Get the fuck out of here, Win."

"I'm not leaving you."

The fae soldiers land across the sloped expanse of Marooner's Rock and charge toward us.

Vane shoves me back putting him between me and the men and women even though he's in no shape to be fighting.

And as the soldiers barrel toward us from the left, down below, the royals are making their way up, hedging us in.

What the hell is the point of having a powerful magical entity if it's not going to get you out of tight spots?

The man wearing the royal military uniform reaches us just as the fae soldiers circle us.

Vane sways on his feet.

Where is Peter Pan? Or the twins?

"Vane," the man says. "It's been a while."

"Holt," Vane says as he levels his shoulders. "I would prefer it had been longer."

Holt takes a step closer and Vane backpedals, shielding me.

"She killed my sisters." The man eyes me over Vane's shoulder, his jaw flexing as he grits his teeth.

"They probably deserved it," Vane answers.

"Giselle, maybe. But Amara wasn't so bad. She didn't deserve what she got."

It kills me that this man is mourning the loss of his siblings, sharing their names with their killer—*me*—and I can barely recall what they looked like.

"I didn't mean to," I tell him.

"Is that supposed to make me feel better?"

I catch movement behind me and spot two of the military men getting closer.

"What do you want, Holt?" Vane asks, his voice reedy.

"Besides justice for my family...I think you know."

Vane nods. "The Darkland shadow."

"It belongs on Darkland soil."

"I'm not arguing that."

"So?" Holt grabs a rock hanging from a chain around his neck and gives it a yank. The chain snaps. "Let's not make this any harder than it needs to be."

The fae soldier grabs my right arm and the guard the other.

"Hey!"

"Let her go," Vane says. "I'll give you the shadow if you let her go."

"You're in no shape for negotiations." Holt wags a finger at the men who have me in hand and they drag me around to face him. Vane tries grabbing for me but stumbles and has to catch himself on an outcropping as his breathing grows more labored.

"On my island," Holt says as he peers down at me, "a girl such as yourself, who committed a crime against the royal family, would first spend a year in the bowels of Pyke Prison and then when you could barely remember what it felt like to have sunlight on your skin, you'd be dragged into the city square, stripped naked, your body used for all to see."

Behind me, Vane growls and gravel crunches beneath his boots as he comes toward us. But he's caught by several of the royal guard.

Holt goes on. "Afterward, when you could take no more," he reaches out and drags the back of his knuckles down my cheek, "your guts would be cut from your stomach and wrapped around your throat like a noose. And you'd hang there until eventually you died a very painful death."

Nausea wells up my throat.

I thought Peter Pan and Vane and the twins were bad.

Nothing compares to this man.

I think I understand a little more why Vane did what he did and why he left his island.

I want this man to suffer even more than his sisters did at my hand.

I need you, I think to the shadow.

Please for the love of god, I need you.

"But we're not on my island, of course," Holt says, his lips spreading into a sinister grin. "I'm sure I can get creative nonetheless. But first..." He looks over at Vane. "First I will claim what's mine. Get him up."

The guards pull me back, one of them placing the curved tine of a blade at my throat. On my own, I'm no match for them. I feel like a bug caught in a spiderweb with no hope of getting out.

What the hell should I do?

Holt steps forward, the rock necklace still clutched in his hand.

He lifts it out before him and several tendrils of black mist trail away from Vane and toward the rock.

Vane grits his teeth together, sweat beading along his forehead.

How do I stop this?

How do I beat them?

If you were going to help us, now would be the time! I say to the shadow.

But it's like it's gone dormant.

Hello!

Holt takes another step and more of Vane's dark shadow leaks out.

Don't ignore me now!

My own shadow stirs and excitement surges up my throat.

Do something, I tell it.

Not my battle, it says.

You must be fucking joking.

Not my battle. Not my shadow. Better if it leaves.

I don't care about the shadow. I need to save the man.

Vane's knees buckle and he hangs between the two royal guards as more blood trickles out of his open wound.

Please, I beg.

But it's too late.

Holt jams the rock into Vane's chest and there is an explosion of dark, writhing shadow.

The ground trembles beneath us.

And when the darkness settles, Vane's head is bent forward, his body limp in the soldiers' grip.

And Holt's rock pulses with the energy of the Darkland Death Shadow.

30

HOOK

I WILL ADMIT THAT PETER PAN HAS NEVER BEEN MY FAVORITE FOE.

He is no ordinary man. And an extraordinary man is extremely hard to fight.

Which is why we planned for the Crocodile to do his thing.

Except he's taking a bloody long time to *devour*.

Peter Pan advances on us.

"Any minute now," I say to the Crocodile out the corner of my mouth.

"It doesn't work like that, Captain. And I'm missing my watch. I don't know how much time is left."

I gape at him.

Pan gets closer, but he's taking his fucking time, probably enjoying stalking us like prey.

"Well what do you suppose we do until then?" I bark.

"We could dance, Captain." The Crocodile flashes his teeth at me.

"The bloody hell do you mean?"

Roc pulls a dagger and darts into Pan's guard.

Pan spins, but when he comes back around, Roc lands a solid fist in his gut.

Peter Pan staggers back.

I pull out my sword with my right hand and hold out my hook on my other as several of my men create a circle around us on the beach.

Down on the other end, the sand is writhing like there are beasts living beneath and the twins are having a hard time staying on their feet.

They're fighting their own battle with their sister and several of her fae guard.

One of my pirates jabs at Pan and Pan catches the blade with his bare hand. Within seconds, the blade is flying off into the moonlight, transformed into a hundred moths.

Peter Pan with his shadow is an even worse foe.

Two of my men charge him. One shoots with his pistol but the bullet hits Pan and plinks to the sand, leaving no wound. The other man swings with his sword, misses, and then Pan grabs him by the throat and squeezes.

The pirate turns bright red as he fights for air, his feet leaving the sand and pedaling uselessly at the air.

Beside me, the Crocodile doubles over.

"What's wrong?" I ask him.

His spine juts out from his back as he hunches forward. I grab him by the shoulder to pull him upright and immediately regret it.

His eyes are glowing yellow and his incisors have elongated to sharp points.

The sharp slant of his nose, the rise of his cheekbones, his entire face blurs along the edges like he is a man with no features.

I blink several times as if it's my eyesight that's the problem.

He's more ghost than man, with no defined silhouette. Nothing but sharp, snapping teeth and bright, glowing eyes.

He snarls at me and I stumble away.

Then he darts at Peter Pan and when the two connect, Pan goes sailing backward, flying over the lagoon and landing in the center.

Water splashes up around him and then he's gone, disappearing beneath the surface.

Now it's just me and the Crocodile, the Devourer of Men.

He turns on me.

"We're on the same side, remember?" I tell him, but even I know that's shaky at best.

He stalks toward me.

"Bloody hell, will you get a grip?"

Then a fae soldier rams into me from behind and the Crocodile leaps over me, grabs the fae, opens his mouth wider than seems possible, and devours the fae in one gulp.

There one minute, gone the next, with no evidence of him ever having been.

I'm suddenly numb.

I stare at the aftermath with wide, unseeing eyes.

Have I lost my bloody mind?

The Crocodile turns his head toward the twilight sky and lets out a satisfying sigh.

Then he turns to the rest of the beach and all of the men and women left to devour.

And he gets to work.

31

KAS

I KNOW WHAT TILLY IS DOING.

I know illusion magic. How it feels. How it looks. But that doesn't mean I can just as easily break out of it.

The sand is writhing beneath me and I can't keep my balance on it, even though I know none of it is real.

Bash leaps forward and grabs a low hanging branch from an oak tree, then waggles his fingers at me, gesturing for me to follow.

I take the offering and we both leverage ourselves into the tree.

Our sister takes flight and rises before us.

"Well done, sister," I say. "You've cornered us in a tree. Now what?"

"Stay out of this and walk away from it," she says.

Bash and I look at one another. He snorts his derision. "How many times are you going to stage a coup, only to lose?"

"Does it look like we're losing?"

"I don't understand this." I shimmy down the length of the branch to get closer to her. "Why go to all this trouble when you clearly don't want the throne."

She's shocked by this insinuation, as if the thought had never crossed her mind.

"Of course I want the throne. I will do what needs to be done to protect it and to protect Neverland. I will never stop."

Bash walks himself upright using one of the thicker branches in an elbow in the tree. "If you wanted the throne, your soldiers would not be so weak. You would be training them, day in and day out. You would be prepared for a takeover. Not saddling yourself with weaker men."

The expression on her face softens. I've hit a sore spot, but even worse, one very close to the truth.

"Why do you continue to fight?" Bash asks.

"It's what Father wanted. It's what Mother would have wanted, too. She hated Peter Pan and he's still running Neverland like some god."

"Tinker Bell hated that Peter Pan didn't want her," I remind her. "There's a difference."

I notice my brother's stance, the ease in his knees, the tension coiling in his back.

"Forget Mother and Father," Bash says. "You need to ask yourself, dear sister, is it worth it still?"

I may have been separated from my sister for a very long time, but I recognize the sadness that comes across her face.

The weight of it all is crushing her.

She was never raised to have the throne. And almost every monarch that came before her has been surrounded by family.

But Tilly has no one left.

Not our parents. Not Nani. Not us.

I feel pity for her.

And deeply sad.

"We don't want this for you," I tell her. "We never did."

"It's why we made the decisions we made," Bash adds.

"We wanted to shoulder the burden of the court, Til," I say. "We never wanted you to have to sacrifice anything."

And it's absolutely true.

We never would have killed our father if we'd have known this is where our little sister would end up.

But there is selfishness propelling me forward now.

I no longer want the throne to protect my sister.

I want it for myself and my brother.

Because it is rightfully ours.

I look over at Bash as our sister's silence stretches between us.

She's breaking right before our eyes, but we can no longer be weak for her.

We don't need our fae language to know what the other is thinking.

Now, Bash says with his eyes.

We both leap from the tree and tackle our little sister.

Bash hooks her around the shoulders. I grab her by the legs. Her wings beat feverishly behind her, but she's not strong enough to hold us all up.

We sink toward the forest floor.

She fights, trying to dislodge us, but once we're on the ground, we want to keep her there.

And our little sister isn't the only one well-versed in fae magic.

Bash lets his run wild.

Honey drips from the tree branches above us and several thick globs hit our sister's wings. They come to a halt as she wars with the illusion and the weight of the thick goop, even though it's not real.

The honey follows the delicate, veiny structure in her forewing and quickly encapsulates her hindwing.

"Give up this fight, Tilly," Bash says.

She struggles with the added weight, panic rising in her face. "I can't."

"Why not?"

Bash and I advance on her.

"What do I have, if I don't have the throne?" Her voice catches. "This is what Father wanted me to do."

Sometimes I wish we could go back and change it. I wish our family could be together again, though perhaps minus Mother.

But even if we could, it would never be the same.

And I often suspect that what remains of my early memories is only half truth. It's like a reflection on water, stretched on ripples, a bit unrecognizable.

We were always dysfunctional. And Bash, Tilly, and I did what we had to do to survive.

And now Bash and I have to do it again.

Bash lunges for our sister.

The honey cracks and her wings beat behind her.

She takes flight and down on the beach, the fae soldiers wail and shriek.

Through the trees, I can just make out a shapeless figure darting through the soldiers and he's...devouring them?

"Holy shit," Bash says. "That's the Crocodile."

"Fall back!" Tilly screeches. "Fall back!"

Several fae take to the air. The Crocodile snatches one by the foot and yanks him back down. His wings work at the air and he gains an inch, only to lose two more.

The Crocodile unhinges his shapeless mouth and within seconds, the fae is gone.

The rest that remain form a V in the air above us and disappear over the treetops.

32

PETER PAN

My relief that Roc isn't dead after all, that I won't have to worry about Vane holding it against Darling or me, is short-lived.

Roc catches me off guard and hits with such force, my teeth clack together and my vision goes white.

I know I'm flying backward, but I can't see through the stars and so I don't know which way is up.

When I hit the cool water of the lagoon, the panic settles in.

The lagoon does not always give. Sometimes it takes. Sometimes it demands something of you in return and I have too much to lose.

I drop into the water on my back and the water immediately engulfs me.

When the ringing has left my ears and I orient myself toward the surface, I swim up, kicking my legs.

Until something grabs me around the ankle and drags me deeper.

The light at the surface gets further and further away and the bright blue glow of the lagoon water turns dark.

Down, down I go.

I fight against whatever spirit or creature has me, but there is no substance to its form, no fingers to pry free.

Air bubbles escape from my nose and float up to the top.

I may be immortal, but I still need to breathe and there's no telling how long I can last down here.

It's eerily silent save for the distant creak of what sounds like a rope.

When I reach bottom, the water is so chilly, I can barely feel my feet or my fingers, but I grope around blindly looking for anything to tear free.

Still nothing. Nothing to hint at the force that is holding me down.

What do you want? I say to the spirits. I know they can sense my thoughts. The lagoon knows all.

Never King.

The voice slithers out of the depths. I turn and see a flash of iridescent light, then it's gone.

Never King, it comes again.

I'm fucking listening, I shout back as several more air bubbles escape with my frustration.

I'm useless down here while everyone I...

The word *love* flares like a match stick in the darkness behind my eyes.

Love.

Everyone I love.

Everyone I love is on the surface and I'm buried once again in the dark.

The fear overtakes me and the fear turns to terror.

What if I never return to them? What if I will always, endlessly be alone in the dark?

Never King.

Never King.

Given light, trapped in the dark.

Never King.

Never King.

I yank up on my foot.

Never King.

I fucking hear you! I shout.

The shape of a lagoon spirit bursts out of the darkness, mouth open in a screech.

The sound doesn't reach down here, but the sensation of being shouted at does.

A current darts past me and I get swept up in it.

My head pounds and my chest aches as it gets harder and harder to hold my breath.

Never King.

Drenched in darkness, terrified of light.

Do you hear us now, Never King?

The current ebbs away.

Flashing tails swim a wide circle around me.

You cannot have light, a voice says.

Without darkness, another adds.

You cannot have darkness...

I am in no mood for your parables, I say. *What is it you want? You want me to be better? You want me to be less dark and more light?*

Just fucking tell me.

Whatever pressure was holding me down disappears and I get my feet beneath me again.

Never King.

Never King...

The voices fade away and the gleaming tails disappear.

The surface appears leagues away, but I swim toward it. Fast, faster, lungs burning, throat burning, mouth aching to burst open.

When I breach the surface, I inhale so deeply, my ribs ache.

Not wanting to linger in the water any longer, I take to the air, let the water slough off.

On the beach, the Crocodile is devouring everything in his wake. Pirates and fae alike.

But on Marooner's Rock, Darling is wailing and I am terrified that I am already too late.

33

WINNIE

I know the second Vane's shadow is gone.

I think my shadow recognizes the emptiness in him.

He is listless in the soldiers' grip.

Holt motions with his fingers. "Get him up."

The men do as they're told.

I flail in the grip of the men holding me back and the blade at my throat pierces my flesh. I sense a bead, and then a trail of blood, running down my neck from the fresh cut. Their grip tightens, bruising my skin and the first bloom of anger comes to my chest.

There are only four men I will ever allow to mark my flesh.

Four men and four men only.

The anger spreads out like fire in my veins.

Before Neverland, before Peter Pan and Vane and Bash and Kas, I sometimes had to embrace the darker things in order to survive.

Sleep with someone I hated because I knew he had a car that could help me get somewhere.

Steal food from a neighbor's house because I was starving.

Let someone carve me up because it was what my mother wanted.

Never have I embraced the darkness for something *I* wanted.

Because I have never actually wanted anything.

It's hard to want when you can barely know the shape of need.

Holt gestures for his guards to take Vane to the cliff's edge. The side where the drop is long and the rocks sharp.

"Because I know how much you love your revenge," Holt says.

Can you hear me, Shadow?

I sense it stirring just out of reach.

"I am letting you in," I say.

"What was that?" the guard says with a grunt.

"I let you in!"

The dark shadow swells like a storm cloud.

I am you and you are me and I embrace you and every dark thread of you.

There is a moment of quiet stillness, the eye before the storm.

And then a vibrating pulse in the air.

"What the hell?" the guard on my left says.

I yank my arm from the grip of the guy on my right and smash the heel of my hand into the nose of the one on my left.

Cartilage crunches loudly and blood spurts through the air. The man staggers back howling.

I backhand the man on my right and he nicks me again

with the curved blade sending more blood running down the front of me.

I barely feel the pain.

There is nothing but the drive for recompense.

I will win.

Because I am more.

I no longer need. I want.

And I want Vane.

Because I am Winnie fucking Darling and no man will steal my power.

I yank the blade away from the guard and swing up.

The man's shirt flaps away from his body, nothing but tatters and then he looks down at his bare midsection as blood gushes out of a cut running from hip to collarbone.

He looks back up at me. "Your...*eyes*," he says and then collapses to the rocky slope of the mountainside, one last breath gasping out of him.

And I turn to Vane, to Holt and his remaining men, just as Holt plants his boot on Vane's chest and kicks him over the edge of the cliff.

34

WINNIE

"NO!" I SCREECH.

I'm running.

I'm running with no thought of the consequences of my actions.

None of it matters.

Nothing matters if any of us are gone.

"Vane!"

I shove through the men, heart hammering in my ears, and leap off the cliff's edge.

The wind rushes up, freezing the air in my throat.

Vane is falling and falling, his back to the ocean below.

"Don't," he mouths.

It reminds me of the same warning he gave me back at the lagoon before he finally gave in to me. When he told me not to run. When he tried to save me from himself.

But I don't need saving.

Not then and not now.

Is he worth it? the shadow asks.

Worth it and more, I tell it.

The shadow stirs again and there is a sensation deep in my throat that feels like something wanting to crawl its way out.

Vane's clothes flap around him as the ocean grows nearer.

I reach out, stretch my arm as far as it'll go, stretch my fingers until they ache.

"Grab my hand!" I yell at Vane.

He grits his teeth.

If you choose me, I say to the shadow, *you choose him too.*

Darkness pulses at the edge of my vision.

Vane's brow furrows, confusion narrowing in his eyes.

"Grab my fucking hand, Vane!"

Darkness envelops us. I can no longer see the ocean or feel the cool spray of the waves.

The shadow ribbons around Vane and me and I yelp with relief when I feel his fingers lock with mine.

I wrap my body around his as the darkness wraps around us and propels us forward at the last second.

Just enough to miss the rocks, but not enough to miss the ocean.

We slam into the surface at such high velocity, the water feels like a thousand needles on my skin.

Vane latches on to me as the waves spin us around and around and the current drags us against the sharp coral reef. I can taste blood on my tongue.

We come up for air, only to be dragged under again.

Finally the ocean spits us out, gasping and bruised and bleeding on the sandy, chilly shore.

I collapse on top of Vane, both of us panting, sucking in oxygen.

"You shouldn't have done that," he says and hangs his head back into the sand.

"Don't tell me what to do."

He groans and I remember he's deeply injured and scurry off of him.

"Get up. We need to get you somewhere safe so you can —" I push his shirt aside to get a better look at his wound. "What the—"

He lifts his head and scans his chest. "That's not possible." He yanks the material aside and pats at his pale skin. "What the fuck?"

"Are you healed?"

Up on his feet, he yanks his shirt completely off and if we weren't under attack with his life hanging in the balance, I would take a celebratory moment to appreciate the sight of him.

There's nothing on his torso. No cuts marring his flesh or his tattoos. No festering wound. Not even a bruise.

"Did I heal you?" I ask.

He frowns as he considers it. "I would say unlikely, but anything is possible with the shadows. No two are alike and they react differently with each person. But..." He pats at his chest again, then runs his hands down his abs checking for more injuries.

"What is it?" I ask.

"I don't feel different. I can still feel something that resembles the shadow."

"Well there will be plenty of time to figure it out later. After we destroy him." I start down the beach toward Marooner's Rock, but Vane grabs my hand and yanks me around.

My wet hair slaps at my face.

"You are not going back there. *You* are going home."

"I don't need to be coddled, Vane. I just saved you."

He rolls his eyes. "Ill-conceived at best."

"Besides, if anyone should be going home it's you. You were mortally wounded just minutes ago with your shadow torn out and—"

He growls and his violet eye goes black.

I take a step away. "Vane?"

"For once, Win, I wish you would fucking listen to me."

"Vane!"

"What?" he barks.

"Your eyes are black."

He rushes over to a tide pool and looks at his reflection.

The words I chose while reaching out to Vane echo in my head.

If you choose me, you choose him too.

That's what I told the shadow.

"Vane, I think—"

He turns around and meets my gaze.

Even though his eyes are black, I can still sense him searching mine.

I know he can feel it—we are sharing the Neverland Death Shadow.

The shadow is split between us.

Vane grabs my hand and turns it over in his. There is a spark of warmth where our skin meets. Like warm honey on a summer night. A sense of familiarity and likeness.

"That's impossible." I can barely hear him over the roaring of the waves.

"You just said anything is possible with the shadows."

"Don't use my words against me."

I curl my fingers around his. "We can debate this later.

Let's go destroy what remains of those who would seek to destroy us."

His jaw flexes and his black eyes glint with the promise of violence.

"Let's show Holt how we feel about his threats."

Vane nods, wraps an arm around my waist and tucks me into his side as he pulls us into the air.

35

PETER PAN

I REACH MAROONER'S ROCK JUST AS DARLING LEAPS OVER THE other side.

I'm just about to jump after her when several of Holt's men surround me.

They're more an annoyance than a threat.

I toss one off the cliff's edge and he screams the whole way down.

Another I grab by the wrist and the ankle and swing him around and around and then lob him into the ocean.

A third I turn into a snail and crush beneath my boot.

I can hear Darling and Vane talking on the beach below and am momentarily relieved they're okay.

At the bottom of Marooner's, the twins make quick work of the rocky slope to join us.

All of the fae are gone and the Crocodile has devoured most of the pirates. And the ones he didn't eat ran off like cowards.

Holt stands practically alone in a slant of moonlight, a

black rock dangling from a chain in his hand. I can sense the shadow trapped inside of it. Vane's shadow.

That's certainly not good, though not entirely unexpected. Vane was already considering giving his back.

"Now what?" I ask Holt.

He smiles at me and brings the rock up and jams it into his chest.

And...nothing happens.

He frowns and tries again.

The twins slow as they reach us and then a second later, Vane and Darling land beside them and Vane looks...better. Whole again. In fact, it almost seems like...

I frown at him.

The look he gives me in turn says, *Later.*

"What's happening?" Darling asks.

"Holt is trying to claim the Darkland shadow, but he's having trouble," I explain.

"What's wrong, Holt?" Vane says, his voice rumbling. "Did you forget to read the instructions?"

He growls, brandishes a dagger and slices open his palm, then curls his hand around the rock and holds it out, blood dripping from his fist.

We watch him because it's entertaining.

"Here's what they don't tell you about shadows." Vane steps in front of Holt and pries the rock from his bloody hand. "A shadow claims you as much as you claim it. And if a shadow doesn't want you, you're fucked."

Holt's eyes widen with panic.

Oh yes, I am enjoying this.

"What was it you promised to do to me?" Darling asks. "Strip me bare..."

I growl behind her. The fuck did he say to her?

"Use me within an inch of my life..."

I step into her, ready to tear the fucker's face off, but she holds me back.

"Then split me open and use my guts as a noose?"

Holt backpedals and holds the knife in front of him, as if that will save him now.

"Take off your clothes," Darling orders.

Holt shifts his weight from one foot to the other.

"I said...take off your fucking clothes."

Following the path of least resistance, Holt mutters to himself and starts removing articles of clothing until he's naked and shivering in the cold.

I like being naked. Neverland earth always feels better on my bare skin.

But there is nothing quite so vulnerable as being naked in front of your enemies.

And judging by the way Holt's muscles are locked up, he knows it too.

"I will show you some mercy," Darling says. "I don't fuck cowards anyway." She wraps her hand around his wrist and blackness spreads through his veins and bleeds up and up to his chest, then up his throat.

He lets out several hiccupping breaths.

Darling pushes his arm in, driving his blade closer and closer to his stomach. He fights her, teeth gritted as the blackness races upward.

She's half his size in height and weight, but he's having a hard time matching her in strength.

And watching Darling have her retribution is the single sexiest thing I've ever witnessed.

The blade pierces Holt's stomach and he lets out a disgusting sob.

Darling jams the blade forward, then drags it across his stomach.

His guts spill out and he coughs up blood, sinks to his knees. He's in so much pain, he can't speak.

"Goodbye, Holt," Vane says and then kicks him over the cliff's edge, guts and all.

When they turn to us, shoulder to shoulder, it's obvious what has happened.

The Neverland Death Shadow is pulsing in their eyes.

Vane is healed and Darling is no longer suffering under the full weight of the shadow.

I am so fucking relieved I could scream.

Instead, I grab Darling by the wrist, yank her into me and kiss her.

I kiss her like I mean it because I fucking do.

Somehow, the myth of Peter Pan has fallen in love with a Darling girl and his three asshole friends.

A different kind of love for each of them, but love just the same.

I never want to return to the darkness alone ever again.

"Ewww get a room," Bash says with a laugh.

Darling breathes out around our kiss and then pulls back to gaze up at me, the twilight reflecting in her black eyes.

"I'm glad you're okay," I tell her. "Our vicious Darling girl."

36

HOOK

When the Crocodile has devoured every last one of my men, he turns to me last.

I should have known.

He cannot be trusted. He already took my hand.

Will he take the rest?

His steps are slow and deliberate, but it's still hard to make out his features.

I pull one of my pistols. It's my last resort, even though I'm absolutely sure it will make no difference at all.

He keeps stalking me, eyes glowing yellow in the dim night.

I pull the trigger and a musket ball shoots through the air.

It sails clean through him and plops into the lagoon.

How the fuck am I to fight a man who has no substance?

Of all the ways I thought I would leave this plane...

The Crocodile comes within two feet of me and stops. His edges blur, but his eyes are steady.

"Well go on," I tell him and raise my hook in his face. "You took my hand, you might as well have the rest of me too."

He blinks at me.

"What are you waiting for?"

"Captain," he says, his voice strangled and raw.

And then suddenly he's solid again and collapsing in my arms.

I catch him at the last second, but he's all dead weight and I sink to the sand with him.

"Christ," I mutter and roll him over. "Wake up." A slap to the face doesn't rouse him. "Crocodile, I'll leave you here if I have to."

I hold my hand up to his nose to test his breathing, then check his pulse point. He's still alive judging by breath and heart.

But the rest of him is lifeless.

From the bottom of Marooner's Rock, Peter Pan and his merry gang of Lost Boys—and girl—make their way to me.

"Bloody hell," I mutter.

All of them are covered in blood.

Out of one frying pan and into another.

That used to be my mother's favorite saying when I was a boy.

"Looks like you've got your hands full," Bash says.

Vane comes over and crouches beside his brother. "He'll be out like this for approximately four to five days. Make sure you give him water and blood. Mix them together and pour it down his throat. He won't need food. He's clearly had his fill."

"This is normal?" I ask.

Vane nods. "We never shift if we can help it. The cost is too high."

So Vane *is* like his brother. I always wondered. Probably the shadow kept it at bay.

"Lucky for you, Hook," Peter Pan says, "I'm feeling generous today."

He gestures to the twins and Bash takes the Crocodile while Kas helps me to my feet.

Peter Pan straightens my jacket, smooths down the tattered lapel. "You'll leave my island. You have two days. You'll take Cherry with you. If either of you sets foot on my island again, I will string you both up from my tower and watch you hang."

I bristle beneath his commands. "This is my home. You can't—"

"I can. I will. And you will do as I tell you." He curls his hand around the curved tine of my hook and in an instant, it bends back into a snake and slithers up my arm.

"For fuck's sake!"

The snake hisses at me and I knock it away.

"And take the Crocodile with you too," Pan says.

Bash shoves Roc back at me and I catch him around the waist.

"The Crocodile" —I leverage him up and lean him against my hip— "isn't my problem."

"He is now," Vane says. "Don't forget to feed and water him."

The twins laugh.

I grumble and readjust the Crocodile's weight again. For his size, he feels like he weighs a fucking ton.

"Go on," Pan says and gives me a shove. "Tick, tock, Captain."

It takes me until mid-morning to drag the Crocodile back to my house. He doesn't regain consciousness, just as Vane predicted.

I am drenched in sweat by the time I reach the front steps to my house and I'm far too pissed for bullshit.

Thankfully all of my pirates are dead and currently in the deep magical abyss of the Crocodile's stomach.

I suffered no attachments to my men, but it still infuriates me.

Smee meets me at the front door and takes half of the Crocodile's weight from me.

"You're alive," she says.

My back is aching, my thighs numb. "Barely."

We return Roc to his room and lay him on the bed.

Arms crossed, Smee says, "Déjà vu."

I collapse into the chair. Smee pours me a drink and I gladly down it in one long gulp.

When I come up for air, I find Smee watching me.

"What?"

"You lost," she guesses.

I sit forward, my elbows on my knees, the empty glass still clutched in hand. It's cool in my sweaty grip.

"I've come to realize, Smee," I say, "that I am endlessly searching for something that I don't think I will ever find."

She grabs a nearby chair and brings it over. She sits on it backwards, arms braced on the curved back. "I have to tell you something."

"Okay." I gesture to my glass. "Do I need another drink?"

"Maybe so."

I nod and get up, fill the glass halfway and return to my chair. "I'm listening."

Every word Smee utters makes me number despite the heat of the alcohol burning through my veins.

I've never been so angry that the anger vibrates in my ear drums. And yet I can barely hear Smee over the ringing in my ears.

"Say something, Jas." I only know the words because I can read the movement of her lips.

What the fuck am I supposed to say?

"You betrayed me."

Those are the only three words I can get out past my rage.

"I did what I needed to do."

I stand. "That's the difference between me and you."

She stands next to me. "Is that right?"

"Yes. You don't think in loyalty. You think in strategy. I traded my sister for you!"

I may be drunk now. I'm shouting, my voice filling the room.

"I never asked you to do that," she says.

"But I did it anyway. I risked my own flesh and blood for you. And for what? Secrets and lies? Wendy Darling is in the Isles and she was pregnant with—"

I can't finish the sentence. I don't know if it's true.

But if it is... *Christ.*

The room sways.

"Did he know?" I ask and jab my finger in the Crocodile's direction.

"He did."

I down the last dregs of my drink and slam the glass on the bedside table.

Five days he'll be out? Plenty of time for me to get a head start.

That fucker planned to keep Wendy from me. I know he did.

He used me, gorged himself on my men, and kept Wendy Darling from me.

In fact, maybe his plan to kill Peter Pan was all a ruse considering he failed.

I look down at him still sprawled in the bed. There is blood smeared all over his face and down his clothes in splatters and stains.

When I look at him, when I follow the curve of his lips and the cut of his jaw and the complex lines of all of his tattoos, I am rendered shapeless. A puzzle with no solution.

I can hear the heavy drum of my heart in my ears.

I turn and leave the room.

"Jas," Smee says and follows me out.

"I'm leaving," I tell her.

"Slow down. Think about what you're doing..."

"I don't need to think about it, Smee." I go up the staircase and to my private quarters. "How many men do I have left?"

I start packing a bag.

Smee says nothing.

"However many are left, tell them to be ready to leave within the hour. Tell Cherry too."

She and I both know that I am leaving out her name purposefully.

There is nothing as important to me as loyalty.

Right now, the anger festering like an open wound, the one thing I want to do is sit down with Smee and vent about misdeeds and disloyalty. Smee was the one person who would listen and never judge me.

Deep down, I know what she did was the safest route.

The logical one. Not motivated by greed or emotion or fear.

She wanted to protect me.

I know she did.

And yet...

She comes around, removes the bag from my hand and wraps me in a hug.

When I was eleven, I had a cat that was trampled by a horse. I held its crumpled body in my hands and sobbed over it.

My father found me, pried the cat from my grip, tossed it into the nearby woods and told me to stop acting so foolish.

I refuse to shed tears.

Poor form, indeed.

I sink into Smee's arms and return the embrace.

"I'm sorry, Jas." She pulls back, shoves her hands into her trouser pockets. Our moment of weakness has passed and we will never speak of it again.

"I'm staying," she says.

I nod. It's probably for the best.

But it still feels like I am leaving something of myself if I leave her behind.

I can't come back. Peter Pan made that clear enough.

"The house is yours," I tell her. "The town as well. Do with it what you please."

"And the Crocodile?"

I look past her toward the hallway and the stairs beyond, as if I can sense him just barely out of my reach.

He is at his most vulnerable again and in my house and taking up space in a bed I own. I could kill him.

I want to kill him.

But I want to reach Wendy Darling first and see his face when he catches up and realizes I've bested him.

"If he survives this coma, when he wakes, tell him exactly where I went."

"Another fight, Jas?"

"The last one, Smee."

37

BALDER

THE WOLF KNOWS WHAT'S COMING. AND THOUGH HE KNOWS, HE cannot stop it.

Peter Pan might have his shadow and the Death Shadow may be claimed, but the island will not be settled until Peter Pan knows his place.

And the man who may be a god must first deal with his past.

If he is to become who he should, he must confront who he was.

The wolf watches the lagoon from the underbrush. The day is early and the light thin.

The fae queen struggles out of the woods dragging the fae throne behind her.

She grunts, curses, drags it through the sand, then turns and readjusts and curses again.

She may be a queen, but the wolf senses only a girl.

Halfway down the beach, she stops and drags her arm over her forehead, wiping away the sweat. Her wings flutter anxiously behind her, shifting from red to yellow to green to orange.

The wolf rests his head on his outstretched paws. Beside him, a forest mouse hops up on a rock to watch too.

They don't speak the same language, but they can both bear witness to the same desperation.

The fae queen gets the throne to the water line and then sits on the seat and props her elbows on her knees and bows her head.

Her shoulders shake, but her tears are silent.

"I will do anything," she says, voice wavering. "I cannot fail again. I have tried everything and..."

She cuts herself off and takes a deep, raspy breath. "I give you the only thing of true worth I have." The queen gets up again and wraps her hands around the supporting sides of the throne where the sun's rays meet the seat.

With a loud groan, wings humming as she propels herself forward, she takes flight over the lagoon, the throne dragging beneath her.

When she reaches the center, she lets it drop.

The water splashes up and the throne sinks like a stone.

Within seconds, all that remains is a swirl of light.

The fae queen flies back to the beach and drops her feet to the sand.

She waits.

And waits.

It's clear she does not know what she's waiting for.

She paces by the shore, testing the water every now and then with a bare toe as if she might trudge in to see if the water will give or take.

She waits some more.

The wolf waits and the mouse waits.

When the sun should crest the horizon and break across the sky, the sky turns dark instead and storm clouds roll in.

The wolf sniffs the air and smells the shift in the energy.

The lagoon's waters grow choppy. The fae queen steps back and shields her eyes with her arm.

The clouds churn.

Thunder rumbles overhead and the bright, swirling light of the lagoon flickers out as something dark emerges from the water.

The fae queen sucks in a breath and stumbles back so quickly, her feet get tangled beneath her and she slams to the sand.

The wolf and the mouse look at one another.

This is how it begins.

And how it will end.

EPILOGUE

PETER PAN

When I wake, I am keenly aware of four other heart beats in the room.

I am used to waking to darkness and silence.

Their heartbeats are a comfort.

Darling, Vane, Kas and Bash.

Darling is lying at the foot of the bed with Vane wrapped around her from behind. She's got her head resting on Bash's chest.

I'm at the head of the bed with Kas on the other side.

We need a bigger fucking bed.

Now that I have my shadow, I barely sleep and I am hungry for sunlight.

I slip out of the bed and leave the room. I might as well take advantage of the quiet and the light while everyone else is still asleep.

Things are better on Neverland.

Winnie and Vane have the shadow. The twins...well, the

twins still need help, but that will come. The fae queen must be desperate now. We've defeated her around every turn.

If it was up to me, she'd be abdicating her throne and giving her brothers what is rightfully theirs. There are no more schemes for her to implement.

All of her cards have been played.

I make my way to the kitchen and to the balcony doors, but there is no sunlight beyond. Only dark, rolling clouds.

I almost go back to bed until I spot a figure on the balcony.

Ice fills my veins and dread fills my gut.

My hands are shaking when I reach out for the door handles and yank them open, praying to all the gods that this is a terrible joke.

An illusion.

I even check over my shoulder to see if the twins are there, burying their laughter.

But there is no one and the figure remains.

And when she turns around, she fills the balcony with light. All of her is glowing. From her bright, shining face, to her bright golden wings.

Pixie dust glitters in the air around her.

"Hello, Peter Pan," Tinker Bell says.

If you'd like to continue on the adventure with Winnie and her Lost Boys, make sure to subscribe to my newsletter to stay up-to-date on the latest Lost Boys book news and get early sneak peeks!

Sign-Up Now!

https://www.subscribepage.com/nikkistcrowebonus

Want to join other Lost Boy readers to discuss all things Winnie, Pan & the Lost Boys?

Join Nikki St. Crowe's Nest on Facebook!

https://www.facebook.com/groups/nikkistcrowesnest/

ALSO BY NIKKI ST. CROWE

Vicious Lost Boys

The Never King

The Dark One

Their Vicious Darling

The Fae Princes

Wrath & Rain Trilogy

Ruthless Demon King

Sinful Demon King

Vengeful Demon King

House Roman

A Dark Vampire Curse

Midnight Harbor

Hot Vampire Next Door (ongoing Vella serial)

Hot Vampire Next Door: Season One (ebook)

Hot Vampire Next Door: Season Two (ebook)

Hot Vampire Next Door: Season Three (ebook)

ABOUT THE AUTHOR

Nikki St. Crowe has been writing for as long as she can remember. Her first book, written in the 4th grade, was about a magical mansion full of treasure. While she still loves writing about magic, she's ditched the treasure for something better: villains, monsters, and anti-heroes, and the women who make them wild.

These days, when Nikki isn't writing or daydreaming about villains, she can either be found on the beach or at home with her husband and daughter.

Nikki's Newsletter
https://www.subscribepage.com/nikkistcrowe

Follow Nikki on TikTok
https://www.tiktok.com/@nikkistcrowe

Gain early access to cover reveals and sneak peeks on Patreon:
https://www.patreon.com/nikkistcrowe

Join Nikki's Reader Group:
https://www.facebook.com/groups/nikkistcrowesnest/

Visit Nikki on the web at:
www.nikkistcrowe.com

tiktok.com/@nikkistcrowe
instagram.com/nikkistcrowe
amazon.com/Nikki-St-Crowe/e/B098PJW25Y
bookbub.com/profile/nikki-st-crowe

Made in the USA
Middletown, DE
01 September 2022